D0424860

SUMMER OF THE CICADAS

SUMMER

OF THE

CICADAS

a novel by

Chelsea Catherine

2018
Red Hen Press
Quill Prose
Award

Red Hen Press | *Pasadena, CA*

Book design by Mark E. Cull

Library of Congress Cataloging-in-Publication Data

Names: Catherine, Chelsea, 1990– author.
Title: Summer of the cicadas : a novel / by Chelsea Catherine.
Description: Pasadena, CA : Red Hen Press, [2021]
Identifiers: LCCN 2020002076 (print) | LCCN 2020002077 (ebook) | ISBN
    9781597094832 (trade paperback) | ISBN 9781597098656 (ebook)
Classification: LCC PS3603.A8973 S86 2021 (print) | LCC PS3603.A8973
    (ebook) | DDC 813/.6—dc23
LC record available at https://lccn.loc.gov/2020002076
LC ebook record available at https://lccn.loc.gov/2020002077

Publication of this book has been made possible in part through the financial
support of Cindy Ballard.

The National Endowment for the Arts, the Los Angeles County Arts Com-
mission, the Ahmanson Foundation, the Dwight Stuart Youth Fund, the Max
Factor Family Foundation, the Pasadena Tournament of Roses Foundation, the
Pasadena Arts & Culture Commission and the City of Pasadena Cultural Affairs
Division, the City of Los Angeles Department of Cultural Affairs, the Audrey &
Sydney Irmas Charitable Foundation, the Kinder Morgan Foundation, the Meta
& George Rosenberg Foundation, the Albert and Elaine Borchard Foundation,
the Adams Family Foundation, the Riordan Foundation, Amazon Literary Part-
nership, and the Mara W. Breech Foundation partially support Red Hen Press.

First Edition
Published by Red Hen Press
www.redhen.org

For my friends, for helping me through the darkest year.

SUMMER OF THE CICADAS

ONE

THE CICADAS HAVE RETURNED. I keep seeing them shelled on the maples and oaks near the edge of town, like a hard carcass, an overgrown toenail. It's been seventeen years since the last batch, and this breed has emerged heavy. They're everywhere; loud and killing the trees, leaving their piss water along the bark and scaring children on the streets as they lope through the air.

I watch for them at work. My post is in the front of the town hall building, operating the metal detector that allows people in and out. A glass wall looks out onto the town park. Slate and shale halve the hills, crowded by blooming pines and oaks. In the distance, the Monongahela National Forest lingers like a stain, dark with rounded, blue-capped peaks in the setting light.

I love the view from my post, but I hate the job. My boss says I'm lucky to have it, considering how blitzed I was on pain meds and liquor when my old boss, the sheriff, found me at the local strip club. He fired me immediately, even though my parents and older sister had died in a car crash only a year earlier. I tried to reason with him, but reputations stick here.

The metal detector beeps.

I turn. One of the town council members stands in front of the metal detector, her hands up. She wears a yellow sweater and white dress. It looks like she's just gone to Easter mass. The colors don't compliment her skin tone.

"Hi, Jess," she says. Her smile stretches wide, head tilted. "Don't shoot."

"You're too old to wear yellow sweaters." I pull her over to the side of the metal detector, my voice echoing softly in the empty room. There's no one around. Natasha always works later than everyone else.

She expels a loud "Ha!" before holding her arms out to the side so I can scan her. "Three more years till forty. Then I'll throw it out."

I run the hand-held detector down one arm, then another. I skim it over her upper back, the soft round of flesh there, then down her torso. Natasha's thicker in the middle with lean legs. They're beautiful, strong and curving. I like her best in dresses because of the way they taper around her chest. "You're not forty yet?"

I run the detector over her waist, and it beeps. After hesitating, I pat her down there. She's soft, fleshy. We're not supposed to touch anyone in this job; it's not policy, in fact, we're encouraged not to.

I feel her phone in her pocket. My cheeks heat.

"Really, Nat?"

"I completely forgot I had that."

"You just wanted me to touch you."

She expels another "Ha!" then adjusts her sweater and picks up her briefcase. "What's going on with you? What are your Friday plans?"

"Twenty minutes until I'm off shift."

"Bet you're going to go pick up some girls."

I meet her eye. She smirks, mouth quirking in the corner as she looks at me from the side, her head tilted, the curl of her hair brushing her cheek. "I'm not dating," I say. A prickle of something touches my neck. "Why? Do you need a date tonight?"

From behind us, one of the aides passes through the metal

detector. I wave at her as she passes through without an issue. Otherwise, there's no one around. The hall sits quiet. The tall, domed ceiling absorbs the noise of the ticking clock in the corner. "I wouldn't mind seeing you," Natasha replies.

"Where you headed?"

"The Stone."

Warmth floods my cheeks. It sounds like a date, even though I doubt it will be. Natasha is always stringing people along. One flash of that grin and she makes people love her. It's easy for her. Like shelling peas. "Maybe I'll be around," I say.

A smile graces her face and it reminds me of how she used to smile at family dinners, when my sister, Meg, would bring her over. They were in college then. Natasha would show up for pizza night, drink wine with our parents, and smile at me from across the table. She was so beautiful then, and even though it's been years, I still look at her and feel this tug, this overwhelming love for everything she is. "I hope you are," she says.

She grabs her briefcase off the conveyor belt and gives me one last glance. Her hair is longer than she normally keeps it, the spirals of brown just barely dusting her shoulders. She looks kind of dorky, this springy-haired woman tottering on heels and wearing her ridiculous Easter outfit. I think of how she was when she was younger. Snarking around with Meg every college break, working long shifts at the local grocery store. Asking me to help write her English final essay during her senior year. Now she's a councilwoman. Everyone in town knows her name. I feel this burgeoning sense of pride whenever I see her out, and this growing want that's finally coming to a head.

*

It's late when I finally leave work, the cicadas humming heavily. The summer suffocates the town. It's too hot. The sunset burns pink on the horizon, casting a rose-colored sheen over the mountains. Shadows slip across the concrete, like skinny fingers. Even with the beauty of the sunset, it's hard not to notice the trees. Some of them are lilting, lopsided, and almost black at the bases. Decay has gripped the town. It's in the trees and crops, the swamp, catching on the breeze. People at the town hall say it's a fungus, but I think it's the cicadas. There are so many of them this year. It's hard not to feel like they want the town back somehow, like they're reclaiming the land for their own.

I drive past the library and the old church. Picking up speed, I pass the bar and post office. Mayberry is mid-sized with around nine thousand people. We sit in the cusp of the mountains, a valley that's almost inaccessible for a month in the dead of winter. It gets dark and still in December and January in a way that feels like the area has died. The animals all flee. The crops sit, stripped bare. Everything freezes over and pauses till summer.

The only thing that made my last two winters bearable was Natasha. After getting dumped back in DC, the car crash, the strip club, and being fired, the only good part of my day was getting to see her in between meetings and legislative sessions. She bought me muffins and cleaned my car off. She always had something to say—a joke or a question. She refused not to notice me, like everyone else.

When I didn't want to wake up, I did because I knew she would be there at the hall, waiting for me with a smile.

I curve up a hill and drive into a thickly hooded section of woods. The pines here tower, hundreds of years old. They glimmer white and red in the setting sun. I pull into the old cabin I grew up in and stalk up the stairs to the front door. It's unlocked. I leave it like that—no one's ever broken in. Inside, it smells like pine and wood. I dump my coat on the floor and make my way immediately to the fridge. Reaching inside, I pull out a bottle of IPA and pop it open. The first drag is bitter, cold.

I shiver. The second pull is like blood—all copper and warm. I take another pull, feel it racing through my body. It's exactly how I feel when I'm around Natasha, like every synapse in my body is going haywire.

Historically, Natasha's not my type. She's too pale, and browns when she bruises. Sometimes when she's flustered, she breaks out into a thin, red blush along her chest and neck. It happens when she leans over her desk to pick up a fallen paper, the crease of her cleavage coming into view, rouged by her movements. But there's something about her that sticks with me. She pops into my head all the time—at work, at the gym, at home when I'm scrolling through porn. It's been like this for years, and I'm not sure how to get her to go away.

I kick off my shoes and leave them in the middle of the kitchen. The tile is cool beneath me as I place my bag on the table and head for the back porch. To get to it, I have to pass through my parents' old bedroom. The bed sits untouched still, even now. I can't bring myself to sleep in it. My mom's perfume still lingers in the space. There are no bedsheets. It's just the mattress and an off-white coverlet.

I finish my beer and set the sweating glass on the nightstand. Then I open up the sliding porch doors and lie down on my parents' old mattress. It creaks, and the smell of it rises around me. The sun angles through the glass doors, the last rays kissing the pines. I stay there for a while, just listening. My eyes close, then open as a whoosh of air presses in through the open door. It ripples the coverlet, and for a moment something like sandpaper brushes my shoulder.

I twist, but there's nothing there.

🦂

After another two beers, I get in the car and head for The Stone.

It's a pizza place, not a bar, but most of the legislative folks go there instead of to the "bar" bar. The stools are always polished and clean, and it smells like basil instead of dirty hand towels.

I park near the library and walk the three blocks in. It's still hot out, even with the sun down.

Mayberry is a simple town. It sits in darkness, a square of restaurants, the library, post office, town hall, all ringed around a small park. No one lives here—all the houses and apartment buildings are a few blocks away. The sound of the cicadas grows as I stalk the streets.

They should be settled by now. They should be sleeping, but their hum permeates, deep-rooted and unnatural. I keep expecting to turn and see them coating one of the oaks, but the light is too low. It's just the sound and this feeling, an electricity that tightens my exposed skin.

I wear ripped-up jeans and a tight button-up tank that shows off my arms and the sleeve of black and gray tattoos along my skin. Warm bar air slides over me as I open the door to the pizzeria and step inside.

The bar sits in one room, separated by only a half wall from the restaurant. It's a big bar, with almost twenty seats. Several city councilmen sit around it, beers in growlers between them, their suit jackets hung up on the side of the wall. I fight the feeling of unease that worms through me and make my way to where Natasha sits. She's still got her stupid sweater on, but now she wears a green summer dress underneath. It's the kind of dress that makes me crazy about her. The thin fabric smothers her skin, tying around the waist.

"Look at you, Jess," she says. Her voice is loose, eyes glossy. She's already buzzed.

"I clean up good." I slip onto the seat next to her, leaning in close so I can smell her. She smells like rich people perfume. It's a full sort of scent, something distinct and intense that I'd normally hate. She's rosy in the cheeks and her eyes have that sheen they get when she's been drinking. She never looks better than she does after a glass of wine, still pert and alert but broken down a little, in a way that makes her easier to see.

"Merlot?" I ask, nodding to her empty glass.

"Malbec."

"Fancy."

She smiles. She has small, tightly squeezed together teeth. Her lips are thin, pinked by a soft shade of lipstick and the gloss of the wine. "You've been drinking already."

"I had to. Listening to you guys argue about minimum wage makes me want to kill myself."

"It does not."

"All you think about is money." I flag down the bartender and order an IPA, even though I'm good and buzzed already. Warmth balloons already in my chest, that sweet burn I've come to associate with drinking. I chance a look at Natasha. Her eyes sparkle. She turns to me, and I turn away, feeling out of place.

"You don't come around the back offices much anymore."

I shrug. "It's summer. It's nice to be near the front."

"I see you less there."

"But now I get to feel you up twice a day."

She tsks but her eyes are tired. I lean in closer, my elbows on the bar.

"What's going on, Nat?"

The bartender brings us our drinks and I tilt back a first sip quickly, keeping the drink close to my lips. Bubbles pop at my nose. Natasha sighs, twirling her wine glass. "There's so much work to be done in that office," she says. "I'll be cleaning it up for years before I can even get anything done."

"You knew that going in. Didn't you?"

"Not to this extent."

I eye her. Natasha moved into this position a year ago, after a man who'd been on the council for over thirty years retired. "You're doing good," I say. "Everybody already loves you."

She lets out a breath, looking distraught suddenly, like I've opened up too much of her and I need to put her all back together again. "Last week, I didn't even know if we were going to make payroll."

I stiffen, then force myself to relax and take another sip. "But you did. Take it one week at a time."

"You sound like my therapist."

I'm about to respond when a man in a suit brushes between me and Natasha. "I've been wanting to chat with you," he says to Natasha, then turns to me. "Do you mind?" He has sandy blonde hair, lavish lips that look almost girlish as they curl into a smile.

Natasha opens her mouth, but I put up my hand. The guy is a bigshot newspaper editor. I've seen him around town with his friends. They know everyone in town. They're all from money and have nice cars. I stand to move. "Be my guest."

I hope Natasha will tell me not to go, that I'm welcome in the discussion, that anything he has to say can be said in front of me, too. But when I turn to go, she doesn't try to stop me.

✿

The porch out back of the pizzeria is much like the one at my house—square and small and mostly used for cigarette breaks. Tonight, there's no one out here but me. I sit on the railing with my beer resting on the ledge next to me. Lights illuminate the deck but not much else. The trees beyond me are pitch black. They sway in the breeze, softly rustling along with the sounds of early summer—bullfrogs from the pond, the hiss of the cicadas, and crickets. Sweat beads on my neck. I take out some tobacco from a tin and sprinkle it in a rolling paper, lick it, then fold it, rolling it between my fingers.

That editor is just one of many who have gone after Natasha since I've moved back. For a while, she dated the owner of the town's hotel, a kid with inherited money and a spotty, red-colored neck. It's always something with her.

I flick my lighter on and suddenly the forest around me goes silent. I pause, lighting my cigarette, inhaling deep. Smoke clouds my lungs. I exhale, puffing a cloud into the air. It carries into the darkness, then dissipates.

A chill sweeps my body. I strain to hear but there's nothing. It must be a predator—maybe a wolf or a coyote, and everything has holed up to avoid the attack. I'm craning my head toward the forest just as I hear a humming sound. It's similar to the sound a cicada makes, that low buzzing, so soft I almost can't hear it. My skin pebbles. I twist, trying to find it. The tiniest pinprick graces the skin on my shoulder, like the feeling of an ant crawling but much bigger. It startles me. I jerk forward, brushing it away. My body tips. I lose my balance and then I'm falling forward, toward the porch. My lighter falls from my hands. I knock my temple against the wood slat and then everything goes black.

···

When I come to, Natasha hovers over me. Her face is clear but everything around her is blurry. She smiles. "There you are," she says. Her voice feels distant, like I'm listening to her through a tunnel.

I manage to sit up. My temple throbs. I bring my hand up to touch it, but she grabs it and holds it away.

"You're bleeding. Don't touch it."

"What happened?"

I close my eyes as she applies a piece of cloth to my temple. It sends a prickling pain through my skull. I'm hot all over. "You tell me. One of the guys saw you face-down out here."

I inhale, exhale. Faintly, I become aware of other voices, and when I open my eyes again, people crowd around us. A flush sweeps over me. My ears buzz, making everything feel like it's louder and closer than it should be. "I was sitting on the railing," I say.

"And?"

"Something was crawling on me."

Natasha removes the napkin from my head. Blood soaks the corner. "What was crawling on you?"

I grab her wrist and remove the napkin from her hand, then hold it to the wound myself. The pain throbs dully. Nothing broken, just the gash from where I hit the ground. I press the napkin there, trying to think of what could've been crawling on me. As the buzzing in my ears dies out, I become aware of other sounds—people chatting nearby, the soft pulse of music from inside. The sound of the cicadas is gone.

"For fuck's sake, Jess," Natasha says. "What happened?"

I push forward. The world spins for a moment but I steady myself. Natasha rises, too, and touches my waist. "I'm going home."

"I'll drive you."

"I'm not drunk, Nat."

Her hand slips to my back and I have that prickling sensation again, like an open wound, but it's all over my body, concentrated where she's touching me. I turn away from the group and head for the bar. Natasha keeps pace with me. "You can't drive like this."

"Like what? I'm fine."

She makes a grunting noise and I think I've lost her for a moment, but as I exit the bar, I feel her hand on my back again.

It's enough to drive me crazy. She's always doing these small things—the shit-eating grin she gets when I look at her, the tilt of her head, the way she bats her eyelashes. She's always in my space and it scares me sometimes. It scares me how badly I want her.

I walk. The street is dead silent. The dark is everywhere. It throbs in time with the pain in my temple. "I'm driving you home," Natasha says.

The heat of her body presses against me and then she takes me by the elbow, leading me over to where her small SUV sits. She's an excellent parallel parker, and I admire the job for a moment before she unlocks the door and I climb into the passenger's seat.

"You're acting weird," she says. "What happened?"

I lean back against the headrest and close my eyes as she starts the car. It hums to life, and then her blinker ticks as she turns into the empty street. "I'm just tired."

"You're mad I talked to Mark, aren't you?"

I don't reply.

"Jess?"

"It's fine."

We ride in silence, her country music station on low. I palm it off, then look out the window. There are no lights ahead of us. The road leading to my house is also the road leading out of town. In the winter, it's layered with ice and snow, too narrow and slick for cars to pass. Now looking out at it, there's nothing. No light. Absolutely empty.

"Maybe it was a moth," I say.

"We have bats around here."

I close my eyes. It wasn't a bat. It was smaller than a bat, but bigger than a moth. Much bigger. "Maybe? I don't know."

"Are you—"

"I'm not using again."

Natasha lets out a heavy sigh. Usually, she doesn't sigh unless she's at work. There, she sighs every ten minutes.

Night races outside the window, dotted with small stars, the shadow of the mountains careening toward us. She guns it up the hill and for a moment, I wonder if she's okay to drive. The trees rise. We skim the outskirts of the forest, then turn left down a dirt road. I just had it re-covered, and rocks kick up under the undercarriage as she slows. Then the house comes into view—a two-story cabin, shrouded in darkness save for the front porch light. It does little to push away the night.

Natasha parks perpendicular to the house, then comes around to the side of the car like she's going to help me out, but I exit and shut the car door before she has the chance. "I'm fine," I say, even though my hands are still shaking. I open the door and step inside. The smell of pine and cleaning detergent engulfs me, the smell of home. I turn to shut the front door, but Natasha puts her hand on it, stopping me. Anger rushes through my body. "You don't have to."

It sounds stupid, considering I want her to stay. She stares at me for a moment, her face blank, then she pushes the door open and presses past me into the kitchen. I stand there, looking down the driveway into the night. The sound of the cicadas is everywhere now, ruthless and concentric and all around me.

TWO

NATASHA HAS SLEPT OVER BEFORE. After the crash, she came over once a week. I was having problems sleeping then. I kept dreaming I was turning into a bird. My bones broke through my flesh and pulverized into dust, then the broken shards walked together, fusing, and feathers sprouted over them. I woke up every morning feeling my skin on fire, and Natasha was there, like she owed me something because she was Meg's friend.

I shut the front door behind us, and she makes her way inside. Reaching into the fridge, she breaks open a six-pack and hands me an open bottle, then follows me upstairs. She hasn't been here in about a year. No one has.

"You've been working on the floors," she says.

"Sanding. I still have to fix the porch."

"It looks good, Jess. I'm proud of you."

My stomach heats. "I have an extra toothbrush," I tell her, as I open the door to my bedroom and flick on the light switch. Light illuminates the small room. The walls are wood and so is the floor, smooth with the lacquer I recently applied. "Do you want Meg's room?"

"I'll stay with you."

That warm feeling surfaces in my gut again. I head over to the dresser and search for something for her to wear to bed. My stuff won't fit her well. We're close to the same weight, but she carries it in her breasts, while mine is mostly muscle, strapped to my shoulders and thighs. "I'm fine, Nat."

"You've been weird lately."

"I haven't."

"It's the anniversary, isn't it?"

I pick out a black band tee and sling it over my shoulder. I've tried hard not to think about the anniversary. The two years since the crash have felt long, especially this year. Life got slow and tired, and for some reason I kept feeling the loss in this yawning, empty way. The pain was a dull ache instead of a stinging, open wound.

"The first anniversary is always the worst," she says. "This one will be better."

I grab a pair of black sweatpants and fling them at her. My beer rests on the dresser, sweating into the wood. I pick it up and down the whole thing. It sends a wave of liquid heat through my body, and when I turn back around, Natasha is slipping into the pants I gave her. I catch a brief glimpse of white, cotton underwear before she's clothed again. "We haven't hung out in a long time," I say.

She rolls the waistband of the pants and gives me a blank look. "I've been busy. I'm sorry."

"Everything's fine. I just missed you."

She hesitates for a moment, and I can see the discomfort in her face. Her mouth tightens up and her shoulders roll forward. She's always been like this. Flirting is easy for her. Small talk, too. But once you get down deep to the real feelings, she shirks and shies away. "I'll set aside more time."

I take the shirt and toss it to her, too, then head over to the bed. I settle on top of the bedspread, facing the two windows to the east. The outside is pure black. I can't see into the neighboring woods.

"You're not okay," she says. She rounds the side of the bed, looking down at me. From this angle, the light above her catches her curls. I want to reach out and tangle my fingers in them. I want to pull her down on the bed and put my mouth on her, to hold her steady beneath me.

"I'm fine," I say. "Go clean up."

She lingers, and for a moment I think she might push harder. I need her to, but after a while, she walks away. I'm not surprised. We've been like this for ages—me needing and not knowing how to tell her. Her and her boundaries shutting me out.

I wake up to the sun streaming in through the window. It lays a path across the floor, over the lip of the bed, and onto Natasha's bare feet. Her hair is flat on the side where she slept. Her mouth is partially open, her chest rising and falling. I love the way she looks without a bra. I love the shape of her breasts through the shirt fabric. I reach out, my hand hovering over them before tucking a flat piece of hair away from her mouth.

In the shower, I run the water cold; it's hot upstairs in the heat of summer like this. I shampoo my hair, letting the water sting my face and cool the throbbing in my head from where I hit the porch. After rinsing off, I check the wound. It's not as bad as it looks. The impact left a jagged red mark across my forehead about an inch long. It's tender to the touch but doesn't feel hot or inflamed.

Natasha is awake when I get out. Her eyes are mussed with sleep and her mouth pinches in a frown.

I don't talk to her, just let her brush by me to use the bathroom. The showerhead turns on, and about ten minutes later, she returns to the bedroom, wearing my old robe. A blush sweeps my cheeks and I look away, busying myself with finding her a clean pair of clothes to wear. I kept some of Meg's—I don't know why. They sit in the bottom drawer of my dresser. I pick out a pink satin blouse for her and black yoga pants.

"Here." I toss them at her.

I keep my back to her, her clothes ruffling as she changes. I want to turn around and watch her but instead, I sit down on the bed, facing away from her, toward a row of three windows. They sit low on the wall, partially shrouded by the roof over-hang, and look out onto the yard and forest. "These are Meg's?" she asks.

"The shirt won't fit my arms. Who was that guy at the bar?"

"Who? Mark?" She rounds the bed and sits down next to me, her weight depressing the mattress. "He's an editor."

I sit. My stomach is tight. I look down at the pants my sister once wore—the worn threads, the sagging cuffs. Natasha's thighs run long and lean in them. "Do you like him?"

"What?"

"Are you interested in him?"

She laughs like it's some joke. "What? You're jealous?"

I don't say anything.

"Jess . . ."

I turn away from her to stare back out at the forest, the grass. The light is blinding today. Warm and hot through the glass. I'm about to stand up when a bug lands on the center of the window. It's dark and large and flaps its wings once before falling still.

"What is that?" Natasha asks.

I peer closer. The bug is at least four inches long with a thick, hard-looking torso. "A cicada."

We sit, watching it. Another flies to the window, sitting next to the first. Their wings flutter, blue in the light. They're much bigger than normal. I know Empress cicadas can get up to three inches, but we don't have those around here. I can't tell where they've come from, or how they're getting up this high. Cicadas can't fly well. The only way they could've managed is if they caught a current and rode it up.

"They're big," Natasha says. "Right? Aren't they bigger than normal?"

"Maybe they had a real good hibernation."

They hiss and the buzzing hum of their wings echoes through the windowpane. It's the same sound I heard after the crash, when the doctor on the phone told me to hurry to the hospital, a low drilling, consistent, persistent. Their bodies are black and blue, and glint in the light.

Natasha's hand lingers on my arm, her palm warm. I try not to notice it as a third cicada joins the others. They flutter close together. I break free of her to kneel on the floor in front of the window where they sit. The wood tile sears my kneecaps. I place my hand on the window.

"What are they doing?" Natasha asks.

I peer close. They're much too large. I try to think of what could've made them this big—longer than normal hibernation? Maybe something in the trees? I go back to the night before. It could've been a cicada that landed on me. It felt like it might've been one.

I hit the window with my palm. The cicadas jolt, then take off into flight. I try to see where they've come from, but they disappear in a sliver of light. I can still feel the pulse of them through the window in my hand.

"What the hell was that?" Natasha asks.

I turn to face her. The pink shirt stretches tight across her breasts. I can see the underside of her bra outlined in it. "It's their time of year," I say.

"How'd they get up here, though?"

"They must've just gotten caught in an air current." I rise, going to the closet to get a hat. There's still this weird feeling in my chest, but I'm not sure what I can do about it. They're just bugs.

The bigger problem is that I'm starving and there's no food in the house. My stomach's been rumbling since I woke up. "Want to head to the diner? I'm starved."

She stands, walking over to me. She's used my Old Spice body wash and the smell of it lingers on her, filling the room. Her skin is still pink from the hot water. "Do you think you felt one of those things last night?"

I pull a hat on backwards, smoothing down my hair. Hers is still a little flat, but I can see where she ran a comb through it in the bathroom. "I don't know."

"Maybe they're dangerous."

"I'm starving," I repeat. "Diner or no diner?"

She stares at me for a moment, and then the glimmer returns to her eyes. It looks like she's about to say something naughty when my stomach growls, loudly. Her eyes widen. She looks down at my stomach and pats just over my belly button. "I guess we should go before you try to eat me, huh?"

"You'd be so lucky," I tell her.

We drive back into town to the diner and she orders a sweet plate—pancakes, strawberries, whipped cream, and half a cranberry and walnut muffin. I get sausage links, a biscuit with gravy, and some eggs over-easy. I stab at them as Natasha slices her pancakes into tiny bites. She's always been a dainty eater, but not necessarily a polite one. She licks the prongs of her forks after eating salads. She'll dip a knife in a peanut butter jar and suck the thing clean right there in her office.

"Morning, councilwoman," one of the waitresses says. She's an older woman in her seventies. Plump with curly, lavender-tinted hair.

"Morning, Lizzy."

"You hear what happened?"

Natasha sips from her coffee cup. Her eyes are wide, eyebrows raised, a fake perk. I've seen her do it with other councilmembers, the mayor, and reporters. "About Jessica? I was there with her. She's okay now."

The waitress makes a face. "No, with James Collins."

I stab at a sausage. Juice squirts out onto Lizzy's apron, yellow like piss on the white of the cloth. I cough and shove the piece in my mouth, chew, and look up at her. "Well, go ahead and tell us."

Lizzy leans in, her hands fisted on the table as she hunches down. "I heard from the sheriff this morning that some kind of bug went after him and his wife. They all had bite marks all over them. Mason thought it might be drugs, but they didn't ring positive for anything."

"They probably didn't know what drugs to look for," I say. "That's why they didn't show up on a tox screen."

Natasha stares at me, a piece of pancake hanging from her fork. She holds it there for a second before bringing it to her mouth and chewing. A smirk touches her face. "I forgot you were a cop."

The waitress stands there, watching us with her stupid sausage-drizzled apron. I want her to leave so I can flirt with Natasha unsupervised, but she remains, her hands on the table. "Funny thing was that he had all these sucker points on his skin, like big ole mosquitoes."

"Mosquitoes?" Natasha asks.

"Well, what else could they be?"

I turn and look out the window. The square sits quiet. No one's out. One of the swings on the playground is jostled by the wind. I squint as a row of birds crosses the sky. They curve in an arc, heading down along the tree line.

"Damn man went crazy is what I think," Lizzy continues.

The line of birds takes another turn, then heads off into the mountains.

"Jess," Natasha says. "Did you hear that?"

"What?"

"She thinks James lost it."

"She thinks everyone's lost it," I say.

They chatter on. Natasha is bad at getting people to shut up sometimes, especially if she's in a good mood. At first, I thought it because she was too nice, but then I realized it was all about the campaign. In college, she never hesitated to shut someone down. And while working in politics has made her stronger in some ways, I can also see the cracks in her, the things she has sacrificed of herself for her position.

A low humming sound catches my attention. I turn to find a stray cicada perched on the corner of the glass panel next to me. Its wings flutter, glinting in the sunlight. I hold my hand out to the glass. A tension builds in my stomach, like the feeling you get before going down a waterslide. Electricity.

Natasha asks me a question, but her voice seems far away. I keep my eyes on the cicada. Brown shell. Red etching. Translucent, wisping wings. It's large, like the other ones. I put my hand up against its body through the glass, and it stretches all the way to the end of my ring finger.

"Another one?" Natasha asks.

I keep my hand there. The humming reverberates through the glass and up my palm.

Twenty minutes later, Natasha sips on pomegranate juice as I soak up the last gobs of oil with a biscuit. My throat feels dry. I'm not even hungry anymore, just tired. The two-year anniversary of the crash is in one week, but it feels like the day has already arrived and I keep living it over and over again.

"Lizzy said the sheriff asked for you this morning," Natasha says.

My stomach tenses. I put down my fork and wipe my mouth on a napkin. "I thought pomegranate juice had too many calories in it."

"Don't change the subject."

"Why did he ask for me?"

Natasha sips. The liquid leaves her lips a blood red color. I reach out and wipe some from her mouth. It stains my fingertips. She blushes and her neck splotches with red before recovering. "Probably because of what happened to James. Maybe he wants you back on the team?"

I stare at her.

"I may have texted him that we were here."

I throw my napkin on the table. "Are you kidding me?"

"For fuck's sake, Jess."

"I don't want to talk to him."

Natasha opens her mouth just as the front door swings open. Hot air sweeps the room. I turn to find my old boss, the sheriff, striding through the frame. He wears his sheriff's uniform—a navy blue, starchy outfit with an off-white stripe on the side. Mason is an imposing person. He stands over six feet tall and has the body shape of an ex-wrestler. Peach shaped but strong. His mustache is dirt brown. He holds his shotgun in one hand.

I stand, my skin prickling.

"Take it easy, Jessica," he says. "I'm here to ask for your help."

"How can I be of service, Sheriff?"

He looks to Natasha, then back to me. "I could use a good deputy right now."

I stand there, feeling stupid. It's been over a year since I had a badge. Over a year since I stepped foot in that precinct. Sometimes when I think about working there, I immediately think of the strip club and the sound of the music that night. I can taste the pills in the back of my throat.

"You heard about James?"

"Is he alright?" Natasha asks.

"He's fine. Recovering." Mason meets my eye. "I got another call about a swarm of cicadas infesting one of the trees out to the west. Two more about rotting crops. I could use the help."

A feeling builds in my chest, like I'm suffocating from the inside out. It's how I felt watching that douche editor stalk up to Natasha like she was his. He had that glimmer in his eyes that men get so much, like he had everything in the world just under his fingertips.

"Cicadas?" Natasha demands. "I haven't heard anything on the news about it."

"We'll notify people this afternoon." He puts his hands on his belt. The sides of his pants pull tight under his stomach. "I'll need to deputize you. Just till we figure out what's going on."

"Why do you need me?"

He hesitates. "You've got experience our force needs."

"What kind of experience?"

I stand there. The door is still open, letting in all the thick summer heat. It smells like the swamp. The bullfrogs croak their song. The cicada's hiss is there, too, yet quieter. "You're a good cop," he finally admits. "And we could use you right now. Come on down to the station and we'll talk."

I hesitate. Natasha stares at me, waiting to see how I'll answer. It's nice to have all her attention for once. I turn to meet her gaze and she purses her lips at me in silent question. Sometimes like right now, it feels like she's waiting for me to become someone important, so she can finally care about me in the way I want. And while I don't particularly want to deal with Mason and everyone at the precinct right now, a piece of me relents just to see how she'll act. To see if things could change. "Fine," I say to Mason. "But no handcuffs this time."

Returning to the precinct for the first time since I was arrested is exactly how I felt coming back to Mayberry after so many years out of state. Everything looks the same, except slightly different. The walls are a different tint of blue, lighter than before. Someone's recently buffed the floors.

Brenda, the dispatch, gives me a hug as soon as I walk through the door, but the other two deputies, Tommy and Junior, keep their distance. After saying hello to everyone, I peer through the office rooms in the back. My office is still there, empty. I touch the bookshelves where I used to put my things and run my fingers over my old desk.

"Same old, same old," Brenda says from the doorway.

I turn to look at her. She looks the same, too. Always in her khaki pants and white sneakers. Hair braided back tight and neat. I can smell her old lady perfume, kind of like face powder, and it makes me feel like I'm home. "I missed you," I say.

"You doing okay?"

"I'm clean."

She nods. "Good girl."

At 1:00 p.m., Mason makes an announcement on the radio that there has been erratic behavior by a brood of local cicadas and that everyone is encouraged to stay away from them. He sets a curfew for 10:00 p.m. that night.

At 3:00 p.m., he and I head out to James's farm where the accident happened. The sun is halfway into setting, still burning strong but on an angle. It sends a long, lean shadow of his farm across the grass where we park. I step outside the truck with my new gun and a deputy's badge. The weight feels comforting against my hip.

"He was found in the crop?" I ask.

Mason struts out in front of me, slipping between dry husks. His belt hangs low on his expanding waist. He's tall and not particularly fat, but soft looking, the kind of man that seems powerful because of the force of his body, not the leanness of it. "Wife found him about twenty feet in." He keeps walking until we get to a flattened section of stalks. It looks like someone fell or took cover from something. Mason looks around, then squats. "Same damn thing went after her."

I look around. Some of the stalks are mangled, leading in a path from the yard to where we are. "It was daylight when it happened?"

Mason squints up at me. "Early morning."

"So, let's say we believe him. Where are the bugs now?"

"They could be anywhere."

I think back to the report I read over briefly at the precinct. James said the bugs came out of nowhere. He and his wife were working outside when it happened. Based on the timing, I doubt drugs were involved. "He was hiding from something," I say.

Mason stands. "He was scared when I talked to him. Something happened. Not sure what, though."

I peer out into the fields. The rows, sunshine colored, go on forever. They stretch straight to the edge of the forest where they disappear under a shade of tree coverage. The hissing sound of the cicadas grows louder. I shade my eyes with my hand, peering down the rows, when something buzzes past me.

My body tenses. I turn but there's nothing there. The rush of air happens again, this time on the other side of me, and I squat instinctively, drawing my gun. The stalks sway over my head, a rustle like shedding skin. My heart beats. I stay poised there, my finger on the trigger. "What was that?" I ask.

From somewhere I can't see, Mason quiets me.

I do as I'm told, looking at the sky. The hissing sound grows. I crane my neck, trying to spot the swarm but there's nothing. Just the surrounding trees and the whisper of the stalks. I'm rising to my feet again when Mason calls out.

"Mason?"

I can't see him, but I can hear him cursing and moving erratically. Then I hear a gunshot and everything goes quiet. The humming dies out. I stay there, straining to hear. The stalks are still and silent.

"Mason?" I push forward, slapping at dry husks, until I find him sitting on his ass in the middle of a busted up semi-circle of stalks. "What the hell happened?"

"Call Brenda and tell them we're heading back soon."

I rise slowly to my feet. My skin bristles, braced for an attack. I hesitate for a moment, listening, but the sound is gone. Keeping my gun in my hand, I turn and head for the SUV. Nothing stops me, even though I have this strange feeling of being watched. I open the passenger's seat door and grab the radio, call Brenda. Then I turn and face the corn. There are no cicadas anywhere, no bugs at all. No one is watching me.

"Mason?"

"Gonna check this out," he shouts back.

I grab the binoculars from under his seat and holster my gun. James owns a three-story house next to the farm and barn. There's a small ledge on the top floor, next to a window.

I make my way to the front door. It's unlocked, as most houses are here. Inside, the smell of dust and mothballs greets me. One of the back windows is open and a cool breeze filters through the space. I take the stairs, first to the second floor, then to the third. The bedroom is locked, so I have to jiggle it loose to get in. Then I wrench the window open and lean through it.

Below me, the corn stalks spread. They sway in unison with

the breeze, a brick of solid gold. Everything is quiet. I can't find Mason. I lift the binoculars to my eyes and peer out through them. A rush of golden stalks blurs as I clear the focus. Eventually, I zoom out enough to search the maze. I spot a couple of them zig-zagging and zoom in on Mason's stupid sheriff's hat moving deeper into the crops. I look beyond him, trying to find any damaged stalks, any ominous broken ones or bugs hovering, but there's nothing.

"Got eyes on you," I radio Mason. "But I don't see anything."

"Copy that. I think they're gone."

"Where do you want me? I'm up fifty feet."

"Stay there."

He keeps moving forward, the stalks trembling under him. "I don't have a shotgun so stay close," I say.

"Always complaining about the shotgun."

A smile threatens. I bite it back, squinting in the light. "Because I'm a better shot than you."

Mason and I used to spend hours like this—him moving through a drug house, looking for evidence, me on the outside ready to take someone out. Police work is all waiting. And then in that one moment, you have to be ready to move.

I love it. When I worked in DC, everyone on the beat knew me. The store owners, the politicians and lawyers all knew my face. I was patient and charming. Now, I go to work and wonder what the point is. I don't feel like I'm helping anyone anymore. There's no one to go home to at night, and Natasha is like an ad flitting across the screen. I see her for five, ten minutes at a time. It's never enough.

I trace Mason through the field. He's close to the edge, near the forest. If he slips under the shade of the trees, I won't be able to tail him anymore. "Get away from the tree line," I radio him. He doesn't reply, just keeps moving. The shadows of the pines darken his outline. I catch a glimmer of movement from between the tree branches but it's hard to make anything out from this far away. "Mason, on your right."

He slips into the trees and suddenly I can't track him anymore. I scan the area frantically, trying to find him. That hissing sound begins again, and I draw my gun up, leveling it at the tree line. It's just the hissing sound and the sway of the trees, and then Mason gives a shout. He fires once. Then everything goes quiet.

※

I was in a shootout once in DC. My partner and I got caught up in a drug trade and two of the perps opened fire on us in an alley. I hid behind a dumpster for cover. The sound of the bullets out in the open was louder than I expected. They zinged off metal, cracking the air.

Sound in DC was everything. It was everywhere, all the time. Here, everything is just so damn quiet. I hadn't realized how accustomed I'd become to the noise until one night I lay in bed at the house and couldn't sleep because there was no traffic turning or horns honking. No muffled shouts from the street below or music playing from the warehouse down the street.

In the DC shootout, the perps ran out of bullets first. I heard their footsteps scampering down the alleyway and followed, running through a maze of trash and old cardboard. The alley was squished between two brick buildings and smelled of diesel fuel. I caught up with them near the middle, where a twenty-foot-high metal fence blocked them from exiting. It was two against one for a minute, and although I had a gun, I didn't want to shoot them. I didn't want to kill anyone.

One of them socked me in the eye before my partner showed up and we took control of the situation. The impact caused some swelling, and by the time I went home for the night, it was black and blue with a trail of red dots where one of his rings connected with my flesh.

"It's not funny," my girlfriend, Lena, said when I told her the next night. I stood in her condo, barefoot in sweats with my hair up. "You could've gotten killed."

"I didn't, though." I rounded the kitchen countertop where she mixed a bowl of chili. She wore jeans and a soft pink T-shirt that clung to her curves. Lena had a thick curtain of reddish-blonde hair that fell in heavy curls around her shoulders. That was the way I loved it, and she knew—straightening it when she was mad at me and curling it when I was good.

"Fine," she said. "We won't talk about it."

She stood at the counter and stirred. The smell of onion and garlic rose in the kitchen. It was nearing 7:00 p.m., and the flush of the day still lingered in her chest. I slipped my arms around her waist and buried my face in her hair. I loved the smell of it—salon shampoo, all citrusy and stark.

I held her there for a while before she broke my grasp, turned, and pulled me into her. She was shorter than me by two inches, but thicker and curvier. I loved the feel of her body. It was strong and sure and real.

"I put salami in the chili," she said, and pulled back slightly so she was looking up at me. The look in her eyes was abashed, almost childlike, even though she was twenty years my senior.

I kissed her cheek, then moved to her neck, my lips finding the pulse point, my hands slipping down to her hips, her ass. The pot slowed to a faint burble. That and the sound of her breathing were the only noises in the room. After a moment, her hands found my lower back and clenched my shirt there. Her skin was warm, like it always was. When she held me like that, I knew exactly who I was, and what I wanted.

The ride to the hospital is quiet. Mason's ankle is swollen up pretty bad and he keeps holding his side and resting his head against the window as I drive. Once we get there, he refuses to let me push him in a wheelchair and hobbles up to the desk.

He's given a bed immediately and after a few X-rays, he's told he has a few bruised ribs and a twisted ankle. "You can go," he says from the bed, lying back with his foot propped up. He wears a blue hospital gown, and it makes him look so much older than he is.

"I gotta get your statement, dumbass."

His eyes shoot to mine in anger, then he softens. A smile stretches. "Get your pad of paper out then, dumbass."

I pull out a pad of paper I found in his truck and open it up. The pages smell old, dusty. I wonder when he last recorded someone's statement and didn't just log it in his head. "Can you tell me what happened out there at James Collins's farm?"

"Be more specific."

I exhale. "During your visit to James's farm, did you find anything peculiar?"

"Yes," he says.

"What did you find?"

"I'm not sure."

"Describe what happened."

He leans back on the bed. He looks so gray and old and tired. "It was shaded under the trees. I was looking for a perp. Then something kind of . . . swooped down on me."

"How so?" I ask.

"Kind of like a pelican does in water."

"So, it felt like an attack?"

"I guess."

I scribble on the paper. To my left, his heart monitor beeps. The doctor was not impressed with his blood pressure, but I know Mason will do nothing to fix it. He likes his whiskey, his cigarettes, his fatty, red meat. He keeps his vices close; they're all he has. "What did you do then?"

"I ran for the corn. Thought I could take cover and see what was happening."

"But?"

"But it came down at my back and I fell. Hard."

I smirk. "Because you're fat."

He lets out a small laugh, then grimaces in pain and holds his side. In this moment, he reminds me so much of my father. My dad could be the meanest son of a bitch. He'd call me a lazy bastard, then turn around and spend his entire paycheck sending me to science camp. Mason is like that, too. I watch him pick people up when they're low and give them the kick in the ass they need. "I shot once," he continues. "I think it scared them off."

"Them?"

He gives me a look. His mouth stays closed.

I lean forward in my seat, putting my pad of paper to rest on the edge of his bed. "Can you tell me what it was out there that went after you?"

He hesitates. "Unidentified."

THREE

THE MAYOR AND THE COUNCIL GATHER to address the "bug" emergency, and I face them all in the mayor's large office at the town hall. The office is like an antique shop—everything is lined with velvet and porcelain and stinks of old man. The space is tired-looking. It reminds me of the state itself, kind of washed up, with old money that doesn't really matter in the scheme of things. Natasha and I are the only women in the room.

"He what?" the mayor asks. "What do you mean an unidentified perpetrator?"

I shift, hands behind my back. Tightness pinches between my shoulder blades, right along the ridge of my spine. "I'm trying not to jump to any conclusions, but Mason is still in the hospital and we had two more complaints from community members about bugs."

The mayor gives me a look. "And what are you doing about them?"

"I've called in help from a neighboring town. The other two deputies are on foot making sure everyone is taking precautions until we can figure out what's causing this."

"You can't just expect us to barricade ourselves in our houses and wait this out."

I glance up. Natasha sits on the edge of the mayor's desk. She's changed outfits and now wears a button-up black dress that cuts off just above her knees. Normally, I hate how she looks in black. It washes her out. But something about the sternness of the color on her today makes my heart rate pick up. "I actually can," I say. "Unless you want to personally take responsibility for anyone who gets attacked from here on out."

The room is silent. I'm both exhilarated and terrified at the same time. It's one of those things—I hate this part of the job, but I love it, too. I love the looks on their faces, the soft disbelief that some dyke is talking to them like this. I love that Natasha is here and that I'm the one commanding this room right now.

"That's what I thought," I say. "And the curfew extends to all of you, as well."

There's some talk. A few members stand up, stretching their legs and fiddling with their ties. Natasha slips off the desk and heads for the door on the right side of the room. They all follow suit and the room fills with sound. "In pairs," I say. "Make sure you walk out to your cars in pairs."

I've been to council meetings with Mason before, and afterwards everyone always hangs around to talk to him. No one hangs around to talk with me except for one of the older guys, the one that was seated next to Natasha. "Didn't know you were back," he says.

"Mason asked me to help."

"Funny."

My chest tightens. "How so?"

"I'm not sure I'da let you back on the job." He loosens his tie. A flap of saggy skin dangles under his chin. "But I'm old-school, you know."

My cheeks break out into heat. I hate that I'm blushing in front of him, but I can't stop it. My jaw clenches. I force myself to un-clench, smile. "Fortunately, you're not going to live forever."

He stands there, staring at me. We hold like that for several moments. Then his mouth evens out. He nods his head, then turns and makes his way to the door.

I stay for a little while longer on the rare chance someone might ask me a question, but when the mayor begins collecting his things, I slip out the side door and into the back hallway. The lights are off in this section of the building. It's the weekend, and now with the curfew, no one needs them on. My boot heels clack against the tile as I weave down a staircase and into a collection of back offices. Natasha's is in the very corner—one of only a few with a view.

I step inside and shut the door behind me. She jumps at the sound, then turns from where she stands at her desk. "I could've been a serial killer," I say. "And you'd be dead now."

"I have work to do."

"Did you not hear? There's a curfew."

She busies herself with some papers on her desk. Her office is not what you'd expect of someone in her position. It's messy. Her desk is overloaded with stray papers, used coffee cups, and pens and paper clips. Red and beige carpeting swirl together from her desk all the way to the window, and beneath it, a row of heels sits waiting to be used. "I'll be fine, Jess."

"You can't just break the rules because you have work."

"I'm staying here."

"Here is not safe," I say, and my voice is louder than I expected. I'm overheated already, and now I feel like I'm crawling out of my skin. "Get your things and I'll walk you to your car." She turns to face me, arms crossed, and gives me this look like I'm fucking insane.

"For fuck's sake, Jess."

Fury races through my body. I move to her side and grab her wrist. "You're being difficult."

She yanks away her hand. "I'm difficult? You acted like an asshole up there."

"I'm doing my job."

Her mouth sets in a line. "I am, too."

For a second, I just stand there. The room spins around me, crackling with what feels like electricity. I'm distinctly aware of how I choose to move forward could change things in a very dramatic way. But I'm also at the point where I don't care. I've spent the last year in practiced complacency, hating every part of my day, looking forward to nothing but the chance of seeing Natasha and the reward of a cold beer waiting for me at home. "We're not doing this." I reach down and grab her wrist again. "I'm not going to let you get hurt."

I turn, pulling her along with me, but she pulls back. Surprised, I face her. "I have work to do," she repeats. Her mouth is tight like it gets when she's angry and for a second, I consider letting go. But then I imagine a thousand bloodthirsty cicadas mauling her beautiful face and my grip tightens.

"I'll arrest you."

"For what?" She twists, pulls. I'm caught off guard, which only angers me more. Then she pulls again. Without thinking, I grab her other wrist. We stumble backwards, into the wall. I hold tight.

"Stop, Nat."

She jerks.

"Stop it."

She pushes against me one more time before her muscles slacken. I pull back so I can see her face, and immediately regret it. She looks like she's close to crying, and Natasha is not a pretty crier. Although she doesn't do it often, when she does, it makes me feel like I'm going to die.

I let go of her wrists and pull her into a hug. She exhales against me, her breath on my skin, and a jolt of electricity races through my body. I tilt my head slightly. She smells like soap, clean and sharp. Her hand moves to my waist, not pushing away this time but holding me there. Her chest rises and falls against mine, and I can feel her struggling for breath. Through the pulse point in her neck, her heartbeat is rapid. I reach up, place a hand on the side of her throat. Tilting it, I can place a kiss on the pulse point there. She makes a strangled sigh. I do it again.

It feels like every single synapse in my body is on fire. Her hand tightens on my waist. With an exhale, her hips rock against mine, but then she's pulling away, wiping her face. The loss of her body heat hits me hard. She turns her back to me. Her shoulders rise and fall with her breath.

"Nat—"

"I have work to do." She breathes hard, and the slip of skin that's visible along her collar flushes with red. "But I'll do it at home if it bothers you."

"I'll drive you."

She's quiet.

"I'm sorry. Please?"

She straightens out her shoulders but keeps her eyes from mine. I glance over the round of flesh on her back, the way her arms and waist taper. She is imperfect in a way that makes her perfect. All I want to do is grab her and pull her into me, to hold her there until I'm sure she'll never leave. "You can drive me." She cranes her neck and a small smile returns to her lips, though forced. "If you really want."

Relief floods my body. "I'm sorry," I repeat.

"Jess." She touches my hand. "It's late. Let's go home."

Her voice is calm, low and even. This is what I love most about Natasha—she makes me feel like things are going to be okay. She might stalk around all mad with everyone else, but there's a voice she takes when we're alone that makes me feel like something in the world is good, and there is still someone who gives a damn about me.

The sky is only lit by the stars when we leave. The parking lot radiates heat as we cross it, making our way to my old SUV. She shoves the precinct's five-hundred-dollar binoculars onto the floor like they're nothing, then smirks at me as she slides onto the seat.

The town is barely lit. I pass the post office, the library. None of the lights are on. Natasha switches the radio on and tunes it to a country station. Guitar twangs, then something awful like a banjo. Natasha's not exactly a hardcore country girl, but there's something distinctly rural about her music choices. She listens to Lady Antebellum but also Johnny Cash. She wavers on the line like she does with everything. I palm the station off.

It's almost midnight now. The sound of the bullfrogs belching peters through the open windows. It smells like pond, the water being so close, and for some reason, the algae stink and the sound of it makes me feel safer.

I park outside her apartment and when I turn the engine off, she makes no move to get out. The building is four stories, brick, one of the older ones in town. It overlooks the swamp, bathed in a glow of halogen lights from the front entrance. We sit several spots away and the lip of fake light just barely dusts the car.

"I'll walk you," I say.

"I'm exhausted."

"I'll carry you, then."

She turns to look at me and her eyes are alight, but sad. I wonder how she can look at me; I can barely meet her eyes. "Are you going home?" she asks.

"No, I'll probably be out all night."

Her eyelashes flutter. She nods, hefting her briefcase into her lap. "I have work, too."

I get out of the car. Walk around to the passenger's side. The air is humid and sticks to the back of my neck. I open the passenger's side door, so she can climb out. She's pale in the faint light from the apartment building.

We take the elevator to the fourth floor and by the time we enter her apartment, a light rain has begun to fall. Even though there are about fifty other people in this apartment building, there's no other sound. I figure everyone is asleep. Maybe watching television with their families. It's just the night and the sound of the rain now, falling quietly on the windowpane. "You should sleep," I say.

"You should stop telling me what to do."

I pick up a half-rotten orange from her kitchen countertop. Brown dots the rind, the sickly sweet smell of it wafting up. "Trying to eat healthier?"

She throws her sweater on the couch, then kicks off her wedges. Without them, she's my height. I always feel shorter than her, though. I'll see her stalking around with those heels and dresses like she doesn't care about a thing, and it makes her seem taller.

"Ha," she says. "You know I need to lose weight."

"You're perfect."

"I've gained ten pounds in the last year."

"Good," I say. I walk around her living room, checking the windows. She's pretty secure here. The large window is stormproof. Nothing's breaking through it. The only thing that bothers me is the door to the balcony. It's made of wood and has withered with the heat and water in the air. The glass window at the top is dull and scratched. It would be easy to force open. "You mind if I put this bookshelf in front of the door here?"

She stares at me from the kitchen, then turns and grabs a glass, filling it with water from the tap. "Is that really necessary?"

"It's this apartment's major weakness."

"I've lived here for six years and never had a problem."

I stare. Her eyes are already glossing over, and I know that as soon as I leave, she'll open a bottle of wine. Her mouth pinches like she's puckering for it already, exactly how I'm puckering for a cold beer. There's so much of her in me, and so much of me in her.

I wedge my shoulder against the door and knock against it. The wood holds. I hit it a little harder, but it maintains. "I have to go back out," I say. "Are you sure you'll be okay?"

"I'm fine, Jess."

The sound of a shutter slamming stops me. I pause, peering out through the small window in the balcony door. I have this weird feeling I can't place. Something's wrong but I don't know what. I check outside.

Nothing.

When I turn back, Natasha stands at the kitchen counter, one hand clasping a glass and the other resting on the countertop. Her laptop is open, and she stares at it blankly, lips parted.

I hate it when she does this. It's like a wall falls over her and I can't read her. This part of her is what makes me daydream about strapping her down somewhere and fucking her. Holding her captive under my hands until she begs, until she's something real. I picture her tied to a chair, her hair damp with sweat, lips slightly parted. I picture her pleading for me to finish things, to let her come.

"Are you done?" she asks.

"I wish you'd let me help you."

Her eyelashes flicker. "Fine. Put the bookcase in front of it. I don't care."

I stand there, watching her for a moment, but she's already gone. Climbed inside of herself somewhere I can't reach.

※

Years before Meg died, I spied obsessively on her friends when they came over. I stood in her bedroom doorframe, peeking through a sliver of open door, or peering out at them on the porch from the upstairs window of the house.

Natasha was always my favorite. One night, I watched her try on outfits in Meg's room. They were seniors in college, getting ready to go out to the bar. I was fifteen and had no friends. I was chubby and mouthy. People at school hated me.

I stood in the cracked doorway, my eye to the slip of space. From where I was, I couldn't see much. Just Natasha's back as she tried on top after top, then discarded them in a pile at the bottom of Meg's bed. I squinted. She had a red mark from where her bra had rubbed too hard and her lower back dimpled just above her pants.

The room smelled like perfume and alcohol, that intensely sweet scent I always associated with girls.

"Jessie!" Meg hollered.

I jerked away from the door, my heart pounding. For several seconds, I stood there composing myself. Then I opened the door and walked in. "What do you want?"

Natasha still had her shirt off, but I didn't dare look at her. My sister wore a skirt and pink blouse. She was tiny. Smaller than me, even at twenty-two. She looked like our mom while I took after our father—more boxy in the shoulders and prone to deep blushes that contrasted with my fair hair and eyes. Meg never blushed. She was always perfectly tan and calm. She snuck me Twisted Teas and invited me to movie nights with her friends. Meg was impossible to hate. "Help her pick an outfit," she ordered.

Natasha gave me a look, then reached for the glass on the nightstand, handing it to me. "It's vodka."

I brought the glass to my mouth. At that point, I'd never had hard alcohol before. The burn seeped through my chest, like a wave of hot water.

"Good girl." She smirked and took the glass back. "Now find me something to wear."

I looked around—Meg's room was a mess. Clothes strewn everywhere, her makeup open on the vanity, powder spilled and smeared into the soft cedar wood. After rifling through a pile near the closet, I found some torn black leggings and tossed them to Natasha. She and Meg were laughing about something, their voices throaty from drinking, when I found the top. I'd never seen Meg wear it before. It was low cut, two straps tied loosely together, leaving an oval hole in the middle.

I flung it at Natasha. "Here."

She caught the shirt and held it out in front of her. The light caught her hair, making it look lighter than normal. She wore it straight back then, and the tips of it looked thin in the light.

Meg passed by me, pushing her glass into my chest. It was scarlet-colored, and when I sipped it, the tartness of the cranberry juice puckered my lips. I watched as Natasha slipped the top over her bra. It bunched under the cups to reveal a nude-colored lace bra. "It doesn't fit right," she said.

"Take the bra off, smarty pants."

She reached behind and unclasped the bra, dragging it out the side of the shirt. Her breasts fell, filling the fabric like God intended. "How do I look?"

Warmth flooded my body. I stared at her. "You need makeup."

Her eyes met mine and she looked at me like all women looked at me then, like I was soft and small and needed babying. Me in my overalls. Me in my crazy hair shoved in a bun. Me not knowing what would come later and how everything would be ripped away from me. There's an innocence in people like that, and I had it. I wore it on my skin like a birthmark. "So, you can do makeup, then?" she asked.

"She's good at makeup," Meg answered for me. "A little heavy handed, but . . ."

"You've never complained."

"You complain enough for me." She smiled at me in the mirror. "Do Nat's first."

She gave me a look that I couldn't understand at first, but then it hit me. It was one of those secret sister moments—a second where we were speaking the same silent language. She did this for me, I realized. Because I was unpopular at school, because boys beat me up at recess. She brought her pretty friend I liked. She sat here and included me.

"It might take a miracle," I said to Natasha, "but I'll try."

Both of them laughed. Meg brought the vodka to her lips and drank.

FOUR

I STROLL THE STREETS ALONE. The town is quiet with nothing but a breeze rolling through. It smells like the swamp, that stink of algae and something deep-rooted. I'm not scared but I'm not stupid, either. I have Mason's shotgun, and I really shouldn't be out here alone but I'd rather that than have Tommy or Junior with me.

After circling the center square once, I head back toward the east, around the local supermarket.

With a flashlight, I make my way along the edge of the parking lot near the bushes. It's quiet, but not dead silent like the town was. Out here, I can hear the bullfrogs croaking and the crickets going. It's a comforting sound. It reminds me of home. Out there in the woods, at night, that was all I listened to.

I pass around the dumpsters. The lights in the supermarket are on, but no one's inside—it's much too late for that. Sleep edges my eyes. I think about Natasha at the apartment alone. I hated leaving her, but part of me was scrambling away from her, too. It's always been like that with us. I get close, then pull back, scared she'll turn me away.

A lamplight flickers overhead as faint scratching sounds echo across the lot. I stop, drawing my gun, but there's nothing there. I'm okay, I tell myself. Nothing to freak out about. There must be a simple explanation for everything that's happening. Drugs, or something. And the cicadas just happen to be around everywhere. It's the easiest explanation.

I move toward a rotting tree at the edge of the parking lot. The smell of it hangs heavy. Leaning in, I scrape a piece of it off with my flashlight and wipe it into an evidence bag. I'm sealing it and tucking it into my pocket when movement ahead catches my eye and immediately my heart speeds up. A man stands in the shadows across from me. He lingers there for a moment, skinny and pale, before moving into the light of the one streetlamp. He wears a professional shirt and scuffed-up jeans. I stare at him for a moment before his face comes into view.

"Jim?" I ask.

He doesn't smile. In fact, he looks sick; I've seen his file at the precinct—one count of possession a few years back, and one count of resisting arrest; he punched Mason in the neck. "Hi," he says.

"What are you doing out? There's a curfew."

"I was hungry."

I keep my hand on the gun. He hasn't said anything about it, like he's not surprised, and when I look at his eyes, they're smooth as glass. "The grocery store isn't doing any overnights until we figure out what's going on."

"What's going on with what, Jessica?"

A piece of his short hair flutters. It's dirty, unkempt. Jim is poor like I was growing up. People talk about him in town. His wife divorced him, and he never had kids, then the drug problem started. I imagine him out on the farm pulling corn from dry husks, watching the sunrise alone, humming in that bubble of a tractor he takes out. Lying on his couch in the evenings, getting so high he can't remember. "Bug problem," I say. "You should go home until it's all sorted out."

"Bug problem? I ain't heard about that."

"I'm serious, Jim. Go home."

A smile branches across his face. "Girl, you ain't the law anymore."

We stand, looking at one another. The same blush I got in front of the councilman resurfaces but this one is different. It's more shy, softer somehow. I force myself to smile. "Ask the sheriff," I say.

"For real?"

I lick my lips. "Want me to bring you to the precinct? We'd love to catch you up on what's going on."

He pauses. His skin is pale and smooth in the moonlight. His hair ridges with sweat. It's still hot out, even with the sun down. Warmth lingers in the moist air. It fans across my face and neck. "Nah," he finally says.

I should probably find probable cause to drug test him, but I won't. With people around here, it doesn't matter how many times you arrest them. Nothing changes. It's always drugs and money or money and politics. It's pizza at the Stone, fights at the bar, and finding someone dead of an overdose in the bushes behind the apartment complexes.

"You know, I remember your big sister walking around this parking lot," Jim says suddenly. A whisper of cold air flushes my back. "She liked her Big Gulps, ain't she?"

My tongue goes to lead in my mouth. For a moment, it's hard to breathe. It feels like a thousand people closing in on me but there's no one else around. It's just a bunch of dead trees, the night sky, and beyond us, somewhere I can't see, the round of the mountains. "Blue Raspberry," I say. My throat is tight. "She could suck down a thirty-two ounce like it was nothing."

"She got me a library card once. I ain't used it much, though."

I stare at Jim. It's almost impossible for me to picture him using a library card, but Meg saw all sorts of things in people I couldn't. "She did?"

"Drove me over and walked me in herself."

My chest burns. I imagine my sister walking this man into the library. If anyone could do it, she could. She took in strays all the time. She was so popular and well liked that it never hurt her reputation. Her beauty made her invincible. Part of me hated her for it.

"Miss seeing her around."

The burning sensation reaches my eyes. I swallow a few times and look away. Most of the time, I do okay. I see her places I expect—at home, when I pass by the high school, the park. But then sometimes, she'll pop up suddenly and it's like she's died all over again. I get this pain in my body that's impossible to locate, sharp and stinging, somehow everywhere and nowhere at the same time. "You okay to drive, Jim?"

A smile rigs his mouth. He is what I imagine used to be a handsome man. Before his wife left, I bet he was a looker, but loss has a way of changing people. "I'm okay," he says, nodding.

"Stay home until we figure this out."

He turns and begins walking away, his shirt tail fluttering in the wind. The smell of tree decay washes over me. "Whatever you say, boss."

He climbs into the truck. The engine catches, then clicks in and starts with a bark. He turns on his lights, then pulls out slowly into the road. I watch him until he turns left, and I can no longer see his headlights.

My neck prickles with fatigue. I rub the back of it, looking up at the sky. Usually the area is ribbed with clouds, but the stars are out tonight. We sit in a valley, shadowed by storms that fall, hanging in front of the mountains, unable to make it over the high elevations.

I pull out my walkie. "It's me," I say. "Just saw Jim Kavanaugh at the supermarket."

Silence, then the hiss of static. "What?" Junior asks.

"He uh," I hesitate. "Parking lot of the grocery store."

Static again. Then, "Did he bother you?"

"He was fine. Told him to wait it out at home."

"Gotcha," the voice says back. "I'll make a note."

I move forward, back toward the tree. It's criminal that Mason hasn't called in Fish and Wildlife yet, even with how much he hates them all. The rot is everywhere—in the trees, the gardens, the farms. I haven't seen anything out by my place yet, but it's only a matter of time.

I scan my flashlight over the length of the tree. Near the bottom, something glints against the light. I squat, peering closer. There, lodged in the mud and slime of the decay, is a single cicada wing. Grabbing an evidence bag from my pocket, I reach out and pluck it free, holding it up to the flashlight.

Cicadas can destroy trees. I've seen it before, here and elsewhere, but I've never seen the decay this thick and widespread. It has to be something else. Something in the water or bad bacteria that spreads through the roots of the town.

My head pounds near my temples. I bag the wings and after another moment, start walking back to my car. The bullfrogs and crickets whisper behind me.

It's nearing 3:00 a.m. when I finally get back to the precinct. The sheriff from the next town over sleeps in the spare jail cell. Aside from his snoring, there's no sound in the room. Tweedledee and Tweedledum have gone home for the night. I'm writing up my notes about the tree and the interaction with Jim when the radio crackles with static. "Anyone there?"

Mason. I pick up my radio. "You're supposed to be recovering."

"Heard you ran into Jim Kavanaugh."

I sigh. "It was weird, Mason."

"You hurt?"

"He talked about my sister."

The radio fizzes. It smells like cleaning detergent, probably from Brenda. She gets nervous and cleans when there's an actual crime. Once, we had a suspected homicide and came back to the precinct to find she'd mopped the entire place and wouldn't let us walk around unless we took our shoes off.

"Said she got him a library card."

Mason pauses. Then, "Didn't know he could read."

I laugh. I've missed this with Mason. After everything that happened, he was the one person in town I felt like I fit with, and it felt like I died after he fired me. It was like my whole self, everything I was good at, was being torn away.

"There's not much we can do tonight," he says. "Just make sure no one else gets hurt. Try to figure out where the bugs are, and what they are."

"So, it was cicadas that came after you?"

He grunts. "They were there when I fell."

"I don't have a degree in bug science, Mason. We need to call in Fish and Wildlife."

Radio silence for a moment, and I wonder if he's mad and I'll have to apologize. But then his breath wavers through the line. "Keep everyone indoors," he says, "keep those two jackasses from getting hurt. Maybe we'll talk."

Blood pounds in my chest. I know Mason respects me. I know he likes my work. But I also know myself. I know how much I've lost, how much I've let slip through my fingers.

🦂

I should go back home but instead I go to Natasha's apartment. The frogs croak their song, throating a dull lullaby as I stumble up the stairs to 4C. I keep tasting salt on my tongue, something raw like copper. At the top of the stairs, I fish out the spare key Natasha gave me months ago and enter the apartment as quietly as possible. It's dark. I can only make out shapes and shadows. Kicking off my shoes, I head to the bathroom to wash my face. Dark circles ring my eyes. I look so much older than thirty.

It's weird to be here in the middle of the night. I've stayed over before, but only once or twice, and it was after the accident. Back then, I felt like I had an excuse to be close to her. My loss was sudden and immediate—no one could blame me for needing a warm body. Now it's been almost two years and I should be over it. I should be better by now.

After rinsing my mouth out with mouthwash, I make my way into the bedroom. It's hot in here. Natasha keeps it around eighty. She huddles under a thin sheet, clad in a workout tank. Her arms run pale in the moonlight from the window. I slip my pants and shirt off, so I'm clad in only underwear and a sports bra, and climb into bed behind her, careful not to shift the weight on the mattress. She stays asleep, her breath rising and falling. She breathes hard when she sleeps, but it's soothing once you're used to it. Like snoring, but lighter.

My eyes drift over her form. I want to reach out and touch her, but it doesn't feel like my place. My place is in work corridors. My place is laughter and small gifts, sly jokes and smirks. My place is the place where boyfriends don't reach—the random moments during the day that hopelessness strikes, and she needs something to keep her going.

I glance over at her once more. I'm still facing her when sleep takes over and I finally drift into unconsciousness.

In dreams, I'm back at the strip club. The lights are low inside, blazing with green strobes that illuminate particles of dust, suspended in their beams. It smells like alcohol. I hold a Henny and Coke in one hand and an eight ball of cocaine presses in the pocket of my shirt. I sit at the stage but there's no one here, not even a bartender. It's just me and the lights, the low thrum of a Rihanna song. The beat thuds slow. It's so dark, I can barely see across the room.

Finally, someone comes on stage. I have that electric feeling I always get from too much Henny. It spikes from my chest down through my feet, burning in my stomach and setting my groin on fire. I wait. The music has slowed down now, and instead of green light, a red one now sweeps over me.

The woman on stage has her hair tied back. A few errant strands spring out from her face, like a halo. Instead of a stripper's outfit, she wears a silk blouse, a pencil skirt, and stilettos. My heart speeds up. She stalks down the end of the stage, then grabs a chair from below, hauling it up next to the pole. I look closer. The red light flashes across her face. It's Natasha, only she doesn't look like herself. Her face is painted heavy with blush and bronzer, along with a thick drawing of eyeliner.

"Come here," she says.

The tingling feeling explodes in the pit of my stomach. It spreads through my legs, liquid fire. "Why?"

"I asked nicely."

After downing the last of the Henny, I place the empty glass on the ground. Teetering, I climb up onto the stage. The scent of her perfume is everywhere—it's distinctly flowery, borderline cloying. Much too sweet for her. "What are you doing?"

She grabs me by the wrist and moves me so I'm seated on the chair, facing her. This is wrong, I immediately think, but something has come over my body and I can't make myself move. I can't stop this from happening.

Slowly, she begins to unbutton her shirt. The tip of her cleavage comes into view, then the black lace of her bra. I swallow, close my eyes for a moment, and when I open them again, the audience is full around us. Councilmen, reporters. The editor. They all sit in silence, their eyes on Natasha. They wear the same gray suit, the same light blue tie. They face straight ahead, unmoving.

"Nat," I plead. I try suddenly to move but there is lead in my feet and mouth. Heat lances through my body.

Natasha takes the blouse off and tosses it to the side. It flutters to the floor, catching a brief ray of light before being swallowed by the darkness. Her breasts spill out of the bra, and when I look close, I can see the small silver threads, the stretch marks, the freckles.

She bunches her skirt around her waist. Her legs are lean like I know them to be, and a roll of skin and fat surfaces around her middle as she straddles me. She's pale and freckled in the light, spotted with a flush of red skin. The heat of her sinks down into me. She leans forward, and her breath tickles my neck. "Isn't this what you wanted?" she asks.

Her perfume takes over. My head tilts back. It feels like death—sweet and quiet, final and consuming.

When I wake up, Natasha is gone. I panic before hearing the coffee pot percolating in the kitchen. Light shines in through the blinds, crisscrossing the comforter. The smell of coffee brewing sends a growl through my gut, and I sit up, touching my head where the wound still lingers from falling at the bar. My throat is sore.

Six days until the anniversary.

My muscles ache as I rise from the bed. Her room is messy but clean—clothes thrown in the corner, but no dust on the mirror, no makeup spilled on the vanity like Meg's. I sneak into her bathroom and wash my hair, towel down, and change into the clean deputy's uniform I got yesterday. The material is starchy and clean-smelling.

When I come out, I find Natasha picking at a yogurt and working on her laptop. She wears an oversized white sweater and black leggings. The sweater dwarfs her, making her look like she's suddenly lost a ton of weight.

I squint and pad by her to the freezer, finding a bag of frozen carrots and holding it to my head.

"Long night?" Her eyes flicker to me, then away. She sounds uninterested. She sounds practiced, like I'm some part of her job that needs tending to.

"Fine."

"I'm surprised you decided to stay."

"Did you not want me to?"

"I didn't say that."

Above us, the air conditioning turns on, humming low. She keeps her eyes on her computer, acting like I'm not even standing next to her, and it's enough to make me crazy. I hate when she's distant. I hate when she ignores me. "What's up with the attitude?" I ask.

She turns to look at me with that pinched look she gets when she's mad. Her bottom lip tightens and her jaw locks, like she's downshifting into her *I'm about to wreck you* mode. I brace for impact. "Excuse me?" she asks.

"You have an attitude."

"You do."

We stare off. I can't remember getting into a fight with her before. Everyone else is always getting in a fight with her but for some reason, we've never come to blows. Usually I can see it in her and I pull back before anything happens, but today I'm tired and I don't care. More and more lately it feels like we are on the precipice of something. I keep pushing her, waiting for her to turn on me, for something to change. "Nat, you're pushing me away."

She gives a dramatic exhale and looks back at her laptop. "Are we really doing this right now?"

"We really are."

She glances at me and suddenly a deep blush perforates my skin. It's always like this with her. Sometimes when she looks at me for too long or asks too many pointed questions, a swell rushes over me and then I'm red as a beet. There's nothing I can do to stop it.

It doesn't matter so much now because she won't look at me. She keeps her eyes glued on the computer. Her look has changed, though. Her mouth is tight now, like she'll cry, and there's really nothing I hate more. She doesn't half cry, or let the tears come softly. She commits completely to it, like full-on devastation. Can't talk, can't breathe. It's hard to watch. "I can't do this with you right now. Mark is coming by later."

"Really?"

"We're talking about how to write up this story."

Heat crashes over me. I remove the carrot bag from the back of my head and throw it onto the countertop. She's had the kitchen redone recently—the countertops are all marble and dark, smooth, and rich. I could never afford them. I could never afford this fancy apartment, or the fancy electric car she drives. Her life is an alternate universe for me, one that exists but is totally out of my reach.

"I can't do this," she repeats. "I have so much going on."

"I'm busy, too."

"Jess," her voice cracks. "Don't."

"We need to."

I don't want her to cry, but at the same time I do. I've had this fascination with seeing her broken since we met. She's so perfect and happy all the time, I wonder if she ever actually hurts about anything. Her parents are still alive and living a few towns over. She grew up with decent money. It's been easy for her to date, to be liked.

There are times I want to hurt her so badly, like maybe that would help her understand me better.

"You don't have to," I finally say. "Sorry."

She stares at me. I expect her to say something, but instead she just ducks her head down and looks at her computer.

After a moment, I head for the bedroom to gather my things. The entire place smells like coffee, thick and entrenching. I choke on it.

FIVE

I ARRIVE AT THE PRECINCT to find there's been another call about rotting crops, but at least no one has been hurt. Tommy and Junior stand over the comm desk with Brenda, chewing at powdered donuts, leaving trails of their crumbs across the floor as they review the details. The place smells like sugar. It springs warmth to my chest. "Where was the call from?" I ask.

"Out near James Collin's farm," Brenda says. "You sleep any? Look like shit."

I eye her. Brenda's been working the dispatch since she graduated from Virginia's first women's school in the seventies. She should be sheriff; she knows more about this work than any of us. But this town would shit itself having a black, female sheriff. "I feel like ass," I say.

"The curfew kept. No one's hurt."

"I know."

"Stop worrying, honey."

My muscles ache. I smile. "Thanks." I grab a pot of what looks like old coffee while the sheriff from Haines shaves in the jail sink. He has a paunch, like Mason, but is shorter and squatter. His hair is closer-cropped, graying. He eyes me from across the room. "How are you doing?" I ask.

He nods. "This mattress is shit."

It's true. I slept on it the night after Mason found me and my back hurt so bad the next morning I could barely stand. But this is a small town. We only have drug and domestic abuse offenses. There's no money for new anything in this precinct, and that's part of why I like it so much. It's got something real and honest that DC lacked. "What's our plan?"

He draws a line with his razor through the shaving cream. Brings it to the sink. Taps. "What do the calls have in common? Figure it out and you might find a risk factor. Find a risk factor and you can move forward."

"I think the risk factor was that people were outside at the wrong time."

He drags the razor. Taps. "You sure about that?"

I turn back to Tommy and Junior. They've finished their do-nuts now and are wiping their hands on their pants, leaving smears of powder along the navy uniforms. "You heard him," I say. "Get to work."

They disperse after a moment of looking between me and Brenda. I turn my back to the window, the warmth of the sun-shine beaming down on me through the glass. Brenda meets my gaze. "People are gonna be wondering what's going on."

"I suck at addressing the press."

"Get Natasha to do it."

I hesitate. There's really nothing I'd like less than to call Natasha up and ask her to hold a press conference when I don't even know what the fuck is going on. "What would she even say?" I ask. "I haven't figured anything out yet."

"Sometimes you never figure it out. You can still give her rules to keep people safe and give them some peace of mind."

The sunlight behind me is momentarily blocked by clouds, removing the warmth from my back. I shiver. The rules are the same as they would be anywhere. Be wary, walk in groups. Don't touch the crops. Let us know if you see anything suspi-cious. I've done this before. In DC, I did it a million times. But now I feel this hesitation, like I don't actually know what I'm doing anymore. "Call Mason," I say. "See if he'll get her to do it."

Brenda looks at me. A smile crosses her face. She touches my forearm, rolling the fabric of the uniform between her fingers. The warmth of her hand bleeds through to my skin. "Still fits you good."

Brenda was there when Mason dragged me into that cell. She visited in the wee hours of the morning when I was detoxing and sweating and crying and wanting to die. She put a cool towel on my forehead and told me it would pass soon, I just had to hang on.

I still want to die sometimes, but I'm better at pretending. And she's still around, laying her hand on my shoulder like I fucking matter.

I review James's case from the driver's seat of the sheriff's SUV. He and his wife were attacked out near the farm. The rest of the calls have been from farms, too, and most of them are in the same vicinity as his. Maybe the bugs are out east, close to the forest.

I decide to head out there while the day is early.

With my sunglasses on, I drive into the light. The dirt road to the farms is dusty, pluming spirals behind me as I speed down it. Today, there isn't a single cloud in the sky, yet the hum of the cicadas is ever-present, along with the boil of the sun against the earth. It's almost like paper crinkling, that soft peeling sound. It bakes the fields.

We need rain. The crops have suffered this year. The tobacco and wheat crops are about two-thirds of what they should be. They limp over the hot earth, languid and discolored.

Soft jazz croons out from the radio as I drive.

I wonder if Natasha has been here since the last time she and I visited. It was about a month after the crash. I was drinking heavily but hiding it well, still waking up in time for work even though I was almost always drunk a half hour after getting off shift. She drove us out here, all smiles and brimming with that undeniable energy she gets sometimes. She brought ham and Swiss sandwiches.

"I didn't know what you'd want," she said.

I wondered why she would've known at all. Even when Meg was alive, it wasn't like she and I were close. If Meg didn't exist, I never would've met her. She didn't know anything about me, as far as I could tell.

I pass the lip of road where we parked before wandering through dry stalks to get to a small creek at the edge of the forest. The memories from that day are sporadic and loose. I was drunk before she even picked me up. I remember her laying down on a towel near the creek. She kept her tank top on but took her shorts off and in the speckled light, I could just barely make out the stretch marks near the juncture of her thighs.

She split her sandwich with me, ripping it down the middle with her fingers to bleed mayo across her hands. I couldn't figure out what she wanted or why she was there. Meg was gone. Everyone I'd ever loved was gone. And yet I had this small angel with springy curls and a loud laugh sitting in the dirt of the creek with me, making me happy for the first time in forever. I kept waiting for her to tell me it was time to go, that she couldn't hang out anymore. I kept waiting for the day she would see me at work or in the streets and turn the other way.

After a few more miles, I take the turn onto the driveway to James's house for the second time this week. He's closest to the forest out of anyone in town. His property shares the boundary line with the protected area.

I park behind the dilapidated cabin he uses for migrant workers. It's closest to the forest. The wood beams are chafed and brown from the sun. The entire cabin sits pulled to the right like it's on a string, slowly winding it into the ground. The smell of baking brick and mud hits me as I step out. It's in the low eighties, hotter today than it has been.

Beads of sweat pool behind my neck as I survey the property I scouted for Mason yesterday. I glance over the stretch of the crops and the cabin at the other end of the cleared field. The shadow of the forest covers half the crops this morning, like a mouth stretching over the stubbly tobacco. I take the shotgun from inside the SUV as I head for the front door of the cabin.

A breeze slips across my back, sending a shiver through my body for a second time today. I feel strangely out of my element. I may have grown up here, but I feel like I'm running through a field grasping at stalks that keep slipping through my fingers. There's nothing and no one to hold on to. I don't belong here. It's clear every time I go out. Everyone just sees how I was, not how I am, or could be.

The front door is unlocked, and I walk right in. James's first wife lives on the other side of town with their two kids, and James is still in the motel downtown with wife number two. The cabin, he told me, is his hideout, his man cave.

The inside smells like overcooked oil. I pad through the kitchen and an old pan sits on the counter with days-old grease congealing. A few dirty dishes sit in the sink. Otherwise, it's clean.

I check the living room, pad to the corner of the house where the one bedroom is. It smells dank in here, like mildew. The space is shrouded with darkness. I'm not sure what exactly I'm doing here, so I rifle through the drawers, searching for drugs or guns. There's nothing.

I head back outside. The sun has shifted in the sky, tilting the angle of the shadow over the tobacco crops. Their leaves flap, lilted by the breeze. On instinct, I start walking that way. I hold the rifle up in front of me as I weave through the sprouting leaves, kicking up dust as I walk. It's silent out here, the same kind of silent it was that night at the bar.

Passing under the shade of the trees, cool air slithers across my neck. I broach the tree line and stand under a fifty-foot pine. The trees look dark, and when I step forward to touch one, I find they're covered in wetness. I lean forward, sniffing; there's no smell. The wet is on the ground, too. My boots kick up damp dirt.

It hasn't rained in at least a week, and I doubt James has been out here watering them. I check the north end of the trees—nothing suspicious. Nothing to the south, either. Then, I look up.

Cloistered at the top of the tree are hundreds of cicadas. They sit quietly, their wings fluttering. I look to the next tree. Hundreds more. They sit in tree after tree. More and more and more. They cover every tree as far as I can see. There's no sound, not even the crickets or bullfrogs in the swamps beyond the property.

I take a step back and my boot crunches on a twig. The sound of it gives me a hair-raising feeling. It's stupid because cicadas aren't inherently dangerous. They have no natural prey except for tree sap. They don't swarm. They can barely even fly.

I take another step, and then another. Then I turn and make for the SUV. Stupid, I tell myself, but my heart is racing. Dust kicks up behind me as I curve through the crops, stepping over a fallen log near the house and finally climbing into the driver's seat of the car. I shut the door and lock it, resting the rifle on the dash. My breath comes erratically.

The radio at my hip squawks and I'm so startled, I nearly hit my head on the roof of the SUV. "Jessica, you there?"

"Jesus." I pick the radio up. My hands shake. "What?"

"We've got—"

Brenda's voice fades out as a group of cicadas lands on the front windshield. At first, it's just a few of them, then more and more and more descend until they cover the front windshield, a dark, humming mass, squirming against the glass like they're trying to break in on me. I sit there staring for a moment as more land on the passenger's seat window, and then the back window.

On instinct, I reach for the rifle, but once I've got my hands on it, I feel stupid. They're not going to get through the glass. They're not trying to get me. They're just bugs; there's no reason to be scared.

You can survive pain, my drug counselor used to say. *So why be afraid?*

I grip the car key and stick it in the ignition.

The engine catches, roaring to life. The sound of it scares them, and as quickly as they came, the cicadas take off into flight again. I watch them retreat across the field, back to the darkness of the forest from where they came. Their bodies leave little marks on the windshield. I spray the glass, then turn the wipers on to clean them away.

🦟

I'm still shaky when I make it back to the precinct and find Natasha waiting for me. She's perfect in the midday light with her curls spiraling in the golden rays. She wears a black dress that tapers off a few inches above her knees. The sleeves are long and have a half slit near her shoulders, revealing a sliver of pale skin. It's a little warm for a dress like that, but I know she's come here to address the press. It's her typical press dress. More conservative. I love her in it. But then again, I love her in everything.

Mark the editor stands next to her on the steps of the precinct and it sets me off like no other. His stupid loafered feet square off on the three granite slats in front of the glass front doors. Already reporters gather. They block the tulips that limp over the flowerbed in front of the precinct. I storm past them and fling open the front doors without acknowledging either Natasha or Mark.

"Well, hello to you, too," Natasha says.

Her perfume clings to me as I pass by. My cheeks are heated; I'm still on edge. Brenda stands near the comms and I head in her direction. "Did Mason call them in?" I ask.

"He said it might be the best thing to do. Said you could give them a good idea of what's going on."

Fuck. I look around the room. The sheriff from the next town over is nowhere in sight and Tweedledee and Tweedledum remain where I left them, reading over the case files with a box of powdered donuts. My chest starts to hurt. I rest my hand on my hip. The other holds Mason's rifle. I put it down on the desk. "Nat?"

She surfaces in front of me and all I can think is that she is the most beautiful damn thing I've ever seen. "You okay?" she asks. She appears completely calm. Natasha has the uncanny ability to look unconcerned about everything when she feels like it.

"This situation is technically not an emergency. No one's been hurt since James. What else do you need?"

A half smile slips across her face. "Do you think we could sit down to talk?"

"No."

I can feel Brenda's stare on me, but I don't care. Talking to Natasha right now feels unsafe. Already the pain in my chest is insistent, bordering on concerning. I wipe sweat from the back of my neck. "I talked to some wildlife folks," Brenda says. "They'll be coming out soon."

"Good," I say. "Thank you for doing that."

I turn away from Natasha only to hear her expel a harsh breath. The heat of her is everywhere, the smell. "I need you to do your job, so I can do mine," she tells me.

A hush falls over the room. Brenda stares. From behind

Natasha, Mark stares, too. Tweedledee and Tweedledum are looking at me now, donut powder on their lips. I fight the prickling sensation along my neck. It feels like it did just before the cicadas swooped down on the car, that charge of electricity. "Let's sit in the back office. Alone."

Mark makes a noise, but I'm already making my way to the office in the back of the precinct—the one that used to be mine but is now empty. The tile inside is newish for the precinct. It had just been put in when I joined them. A large window splays sunlight across an empty desk. I sit on it and cross my arms, mirroring Natasha. She shuts the door behind her. "Where were you?" she asks.

"I went back to James Collins' place."

"Did you find anything?"

"I'm not at liberty to say."

Her face is blank. I wish I could do something to get her to feel again, to let me in, even if it's just shallow flirting. "You went by yourself?"

"I had the rifle. I'm a pretty good shot."

She stands there in her stupid black dress with her stupid arms crossed under her chest. Her hair is extra springy, which means she recently washed it. She's not wearing lipstick, but I can see a glimmer from her chapstick. "So, what's your story? Killer bugs?"

"They swarmed when I was out at the farm."

"Did anyone else see what happened?"

"No."

Natasha touches her mouth with her fingertips, then turns to the side. A smattering of brown freckles edges her lip. "I need more than that, Jess."

"I can't give you more. Just tell people to stay away from the forest. Same as before."

"But this isn't the same as before," she says. Her face changes.

She drops some of the stiffness and her eyebrows release some of their tension. "Some of them landed on my window this morning."

"Near dawn?"

"No, later. Just as I was leaving to come here."

I shift on the desk. It creaks under my weight. "I saw thousands of them out at James's place. Never seen so many before."

"Is that normal?"

"I don't think so."

She presses her lips together. The chapstick glimmers. "So, we tell everyone to spray their trees, their houses, their yards."

I sit there.

"At least it'll keep them away from the town."

The room smells like dust. I remember working twenty-four- and forty-eight-hour shifts here. Changing in the middle of the room, shoving protein bars down my throat. "I'm glad you're here," I say.

"You just saw me."

"So? I can't miss you?"

The words sound pathetic and I'm annoyed with myself as soon as they leave my mouth. I straighten my back, stand so we're face to face. In this light, her freckles are everywhere. It occurs to me that I never look at her this close. I'm always looking beyond her, to the side of her, worried what she'll see if she catches me. "I guess the jig's up," she says.

I cock my head. She's smiling in a way I can't place. This is what frustrates me the most about her—I can never tell where she's coming from. I know at work when she's had a bad day, but I can never tell when she's sick of me, or when she wants comfort, or when she's flirting, if she's flirting. "Jig's up," I say. "Go tell everyone I don't know what the hell I'm doing."

She makes a tsking sound and smiles. "You know exactly what you're doing, Jess."

"What's that supposed to mean?"

"It means you're a lot smarter than you give yourself credit for."

Sunlight falls along the back of my leg in a strip through the window. I glance down at it, then back up to her. She holds my gaze for a few seconds before I look away. "You have no idea what it's like here," I say.

"I know exactly what it's like."

"People like you here."

"No." Her neck flushes red. "Every single man on that council is sick to death of me."

"They respect you, though. They know your name."

She licks her lips. She runs her fingertip across the dust that's collected on the desk. I could argue with her until I was blue in the face, and she'd never get it. She'll never get me. She has so much privilege here—she came from a good, middle-class family. She's friends with all the right people. She's pretty, healthy, wealthy. She will never understand what it's like to be on this side of things.

SIX

NATASHA FACES THE PRESS with Mark at her side, and I have to admit they make a cute couple, even though she and I would be cuter. While Mark is handsome, he is laughably tall, and roundish like an ex-football player. Hulking enough to be oafish. He's nice too. Everyone likes him, which makes me hate him more.

I stand near the back of the crowd as they speak. Natasha looks uncomfortable, like she always does when she talks to the press. Her eyes are wide, and she squeezes the podium with both hands.

If I were Mark, I'd stand a little closer to her, just in case she needed some support, or just to let her know someone was by her side. If I had a chance to be with her, I'd do lots of things differently. I'd sell the house and buy a new one closer to town. I'd make sure Mason hired me back, and then in the mornings before my shifts, I'd bring her tea and crullers from the bakery down the street so she wouldn't be nervous for her public speaking gigs. I'd do other things, too. I'd learn to cook. I'd make her things from across the world—tapas from Spain and Mexican tortas. And if she didn't like that, I'd figure something else out. I'd do just about anything if she'd give me the chance.

"Fish and Wildlife experts are being consulted as we speak," she says. "We hope to know more by the end of the day. For now, the advice remains the same. Stay indoors in the mornings and evenings, when the cicadas are most active."

My eyes gloss across the crowd. Everyone here really does look the same. The male reporters all wear suits, even in the midday heat. They sweat with their pencils and pads of paper in front of their noses. Most are middle-aged. There are few women, and the ones I do see are big shots—anchors of the local morning and late show. They're all dressed nicely and there's an ease about their stature.

It's funny to look at them and think they are from the same town as people like me and people like Jim Kavanaugh. There's just a different look to us. I'm not sure what it is. Maybe we're more tired. I see it in Brenda sometimes, but she always pushes through. People like me and Jim, there is this gauntness to us. Like the world has been sucked dry of joy and we don't know where to find it anymore.

The grocery store sells out of PEST RID, so I order some online and overnight it, even though I doubt it'll help. I drive home alone, watching the trees race past me. They lumber, red and white, pocked with age and weather and sun. I love these trees. They're skinny, but strong. My mom loved them, too. She'd come out here in the summer and touch the peeling bark. She picked wild grasses and flowers and stuck them in soups. She washed our clothes outside with baking soda. My mom was happy, like Meg. I took after Dad. I worried as a child and cried most days after school.

"You keep finding reasons to be unhappy, silly," Meg always said.

I pull into the driveway. By then, Natasha has long since finished the press conference. I picture her at her apartment on the fourth floor, changing into an oversized sweater and leggings. I picture her pouring a glass of wine. I picture her inviting Mark into the apartment, sweat on his brow. Him stepping into her. Her rolling up her sleeves, laughing. Natasha has the fullest, most beautiful laugh. It fills the room.

I slam the car door shut, head straight for the fridge, take out an IPA, and open it. Technically, I'm still on call. But the Haines sheriff is still there, so everything is taken care of for the most part, unless there's an emergency. I figure I've earned this beer.

I drink it fast. Half the can in one go. I haven't eaten in a while and the buzz goes straight to my head, just like I like. That's why I loved coke so much—it went to my head right away. It was like a shot of espresso, and then the whole confusing world looked clearer. Life was a bit brighter on it. The colors were more colorful, the joys were more joyful.

I drink the rest of the beer even though it's not very good. Then I grab another from the fridge. The house is so silent, so still. I hate living like this, in the trail of where I used to be. I just don't understand what is wrong with me that I can't make it work. Why I'm still here and everyone else has moved forward, and I'm still stuck on these three funerals, this job, this girl with this dorky, springy hair.

After a while, I pull out my phone to text her but then I put it away.

Eventually, I take a seat on the porch. I sit out there for a long time just watching the changing shadows as the sun lowers. My ass sinks into the wood, and the sound of the crickets and cicadas and bullfrogs swarms over me.

I close my eyes and listen. Cicadas really are amazing. They stay in hiding for so long, only emerging when they're ready. They breed, they eat, they sleep. They do exactly what they need and never let anything get in their way. I envy them. I walk around town with this block on my shoulders, this weight of knowing what I am, and what is impossible to accomplish.

I drink three more beers. When I'm done, I crumple their aluminum into a recycling can near the door. I've decided that to end all this, I need to spray the bugs out on the eastern edge of James's field. So, I walkie in to Mason and tell him.

"How would that be safe?" he asks. "Explain."

"It would be safe because I would be safe about it."

Mason sighs. Outside, the crickets bite the air with their song. It's cooled considerably from the heat of the day and I linger in the kitchen with the windows open, letting the smell of the pines come through. The sound of the branches creaking is almost like a whisper. "We're not gonna get all James Dean on this now."

"There are a hundred thousand of those fuckers in that forest, Mason. That's not healthy."

He's quiet for a moment, then, "We've already talked with Fish and Wildlife. They'll take a look."

The sun sets outside, pink on the edge of the mountains. I can only see a smidgen of it. The rest of the view is clouded by trees. They stand like knives over the house. "Fine," I say. "Thanks."

I put the walkie on the countertop and head back outside. There's this raw energy in me, this need to move, to do something. I can't sit here all night, so I've just decided I'm going out to James's to end all of this now, when my phone vibrates in my jean pocket. It's Natasha. *Where are you?*

My face heats. I itch for another beer. *Off-duty.*

She waits for a while. Then, *I need to talk to you about something. Can you come over?*

Can I come over? I laugh, look out the window. After a while, my phone lights up again.

Mark is gone.

I finish my beer, crumpling the can. After pacing back and forth around the kitchen table, I decide to wash up before heading over there. Climbing into the glass-tiled shower, burning hot water sprays my skin. I shave my legs, scrub my neck free of sweat. The sun sets while I'm there, and as I'm changing into clean clothes, I catch a glimmer of something florescent in the window. I peer outside, searching, but there's only darkness.

***

The trees blur as I speed down the dirt road to town to Natasha's apartment. It's chilly out. Something sharp rides the air. I drive with the windows down, trying to sober up in the coldness of the night. It presses over my face, my mouth, rushing up my nose like a wave. My eyes sting.

By the time I knock on Natasha's door, I'm sober enough to be nervous. I glance down at my jeans; they look dingy and my top is too short. It shows off the lip of skin above my waistline. I tug it down as the door swings open.

Natasha stands in front of me in an oversized T-shirt and capri leggings. She's not wearing a bra. The outline of her breasts is visible through the shirt—the curve, the nipple. I force myself to meet her gaze a moment too late and flush. "Hi."

She grins at me, her eyes glazed. She's been drinking, too. "You're cute," she says. "I like you."

I tilt my head. "You can't say that to me. I'm a lesbian."

She laughs and moves away from the door. I step inside. The space smells like tomato and something tart and earthy like oregano. She's a great cook but I've never gotten her to admit it, much less cook for me with any regularity.

"What happened to Mark?" I ask.

"I spend all week talking to people. You think I want to talk to them at home?"

"Why'd you ask me over, then?"

She turns. "I needed to see you."

A bottle of open Chianti rests on the countertop. I walk over to it and bring the bottle to my lips. The wine is expensive and tastes faintly of tomato. I take a couple good chugs and set it back down on the table. Natasha leans against the end of the kitchen countertop, her hand clasped around a half-empty wine glass. "Why did you need to see me?" I ask. A smile slips across my lips even though I don't want it to.

She puts the glass on the countertop. She has that playful look she gets sometimes and it's hard for me to reconcile how she can be both so hard and closed-off at certain times and so sweet and cheeky at others. "Mason told me he wants to get you back on the force."

"Yeah, only if I solve this case."

"He misses you. You were a good cop."

I catch her eye. "What's going on, Nat? Why am I here?"

The smile stays on her face, but I can see her fighting the expression. Her eyes go to the floor. She blusters for a few seconds before standing up straight. Her hands go to the T-shirt hem. Then she pulls the shirt over her head.

At first, I don't know what's happening. My breath leaves my body and I think for a moment that maybe she hit her head and is confused. But then my eyes move to her chest. Her breasts are perfect. She's soft all over. "What are you doing?" I ask.

Natasha moves closer to me, placing the shirt on the countertop. I keep my eyes there, on it. "Isn't this what you want?" she asks.

My eyes stay on the shirt for another second before I allow them to trail up her torso and to her chest. I skim over her body, every bone, crease, and freckle, hyperaware of her gaze on me. She looks so confident, even with the faint blush snaking up her neck, and it's so much like the dream but different, too. It's like I can feel her leaving me already, even before I place a hand on her neck and pull her into me.

I stumble getting her to the bed. She's more forward than I imagined, grabbing at the waistline of my jeans, tugging my zipper down. My body almost can't compute with what's happening and for a second, I think I might be having a stroke.

She breathes hard, her curls limp on her shoulders. Faint sweat pastes along her hairline. I look down at her. She lies on the bed, hands up by her head. I tug her pants down her legs, running my hands over her skin, the freckles and marks, all the way up to her stomach. Her breasts are perfect in a way I didn't allow myself to imagine, and suddenly I'm hungry like I haven't been in years. With one hand, I trace over her nipple. She shivers and it hits me somewhere I can't explain. I didn't think I could feel like this again. After Lena left me and then the crash, the club, the job. It was like the world turned gray and now it's alive again.

SEVEN

LENA WAS TWENTY YEARS OLDER THAN ME. She was like Natasha in so many ways. Her mood yoyoed back and forth. Some mornings, I couldn't tell if she was going to aggressively make out with me or stop speaking to me for the entire day. She stalked around in heels like Natasha, huffing and puffing about real estate, the price of milk, and just about anything else that bothered her.

For a long time after Lena left, I didn't think I'd ever be able to move on. My love for her was all-encompassing. Losing her felt like an organ had been plucked from my body.

I get that same feeling now, looking down at Natasha's sleeping form. The sun has already risen and beams in through the window, rays splaying across the blue sheets. The comforter lies wrinkled at our feet. She's still nude, her back exposed to me, and from where I lay, I can count the freckles along her spine, the soft ridges and swell of flesh over bone.

After she fell asleep last night, her phone lit up on the night stand. It was Mark. I glanced at it and caught the first words of the message. *Don't be mad, babe . . .* Then the green message screen went black and I was too scared to turn it back on again.

I rise out of the bed, careful not to wake her, and pad into the kitchen, pulling my clothes on as I pass the discarded pieces in the hallway. The coffee pot sits on the kitchen countertop and I fill it with ground coffee. Dark roast, from Vermont. The smell of it disperses throughout the room.

I'm not sure what I expected of last night, or what I should expect moving forward. I've seen Natasha at work and the bar. She smiles and flirts with everyone. She gets that look in her eyes, that slow, easy grin that tweaks her mouth, and no one can say no to her.

But things feel different with us. I know her better. I know how, when she's nervous, she pulls her jacket tight over her neck, fidgeting with the buttons, and how she's always late for everything. How she doesn't like to talk to in the morning, and how she hates dirt, smoothing her fingertip across a dusty surface at the diner or over a railing at work. Lilies make her allergies act up and when she leaves her office for meetings, she usually returns at least twice because she's forgotten something.

Still, the things I don't know outweigh the things I do. I don't know what her favorite food is, or where she wants to end up in the world. I don't know how often she sees her sister, a woman living a mere thirty-minute drive away in good weather but who rarely speaks to her.

The coffee pot burbles. I pour half a cup's worth and head for the windows. I'm due at the precinct in an hour. Mason has lifted the curfew but there's still a warning out for people to stay in groups if traveling at night.

Five days now until the anniversary.

A haze of heat hangs over the trees outside. Some of them brown, drooping at the ends of their branches. And while I've seen cicadas kill many a tree in childhood, it's never been like this before. This is everywhere. It's like the rot of them is seeping out of the ground and into the heart of the town.

I'm just about to clean up in the bathroom when I notice something near the balcony door. At first, it's just a low buzzing, the sound a bee makes when sucking nectar from a flower. Then it becomes more of a steady thump. I head over to the door and look through the glass window. A single cicada thumps at the pane, over and over, trying to get inside.

I dart into the kitchen and grab a mason jar from the top shelf of the kitchen cabinet, then head back to the balcony. I slip through the door, my heart pounding in my neck. I open the mason jar and stand there, waiting for the stupid thing to stop banging itself against the glass so I can catch it. Finally, it lands, and its wings tuck into its body. I slip the mason jar over it. It bangs against the side. I'm slipping the bottom over the opening when Natasha appears on the other side of the door. "What are you doing?"

I screw the lid on, cicada inside. "Bringing him in for testing."

She wears a pink robe made of shimmery satin material. My eyes catch on her chest where the material dips to reveal the tip of her cleavage. "Who's testing him?"

"Fish and Wildlife."

She's quiet. I cross in front of her, re-entering the apartment. It smells like coffee. Sunlight, unfettered by clouds, warms the tile floor. I place the jar on the kitchen countertop and turn to face her. She's gorgeous. Really beautiful. Her eyes are soft when she's tired, and without makeup, her freckles stand out more. "I'm just gonna wash up and then I'll go."

She nods. "I have an appropriations meeting at nine."

I search for some meaning in her face, some sign of life, but she's gone under like she does so much. I can't tell if she regrets last night, or if she's happy about it, or what it meant. "Did you even want this or were you just mad at Mark?"

Natasha stills, staring at me. Her lower lip trembles for a moment, then her jaw sets. I can almost tell what's coming before she even says it. "Can we talk about this later? I've got to get ready."

It's Monday morning, a slow day at the town hall. "I need to know," I say. The cicada bangs at the glass on the table. "Please talk to me."

"What do you want me to say?"

"I want you to say you like me and you want me around more."

"I like you," she says. Her lip curls. Classic mean girl. "You know that."

Heat licks at my throat. She stands with her arms crossed under her breasts, and I realize then that I'll never get a good answer from her. She'll tell me a million times how she adores me, and how I'm good for this town, and how I matter. And then she'll run off with her councilmen, the guys in suits, the editors, the big wigs, the people who walk into a restaurant and know which wines to order and how to eat lobster. It's never going to be all-in for her, like it is for me.

"I've always tried to be there for you, Jess."

I nod. My cicada bangs against his prison. He's at least four inches long, maybe five. Almost the full length of the jar. "You have been there."

"You expect a lot."

"I just want you. That's it."

She exhales. I wish one of us was the touchy-feely type. Because then I could reach out and touch her and maybe this would feel better. I'd tell her I love her and that I want to try this, that I think we could push past everything that's different between us and find something good. But we are both so damn similar. She'll never reach out first, not unless she's drunk, and I won't either.

🦗

I get to the precinct fifteen minutes early. My head is throbbing, and I'm so angry and sad I really just want to pound the shit out of something. Instead, I storm into the main room and drop the jar with the cicada on Mason's desk. He sits there with a cigarette behind his ear and his twisted ankle propped up on a stool, wrapped in a splint. He smells kind of like a hospital—antiseptic and cleaning supplies.

"The fuck is that?" he says.

"What's it look like?"

He arches an eyebrow. "How'd you get it?"

"I got lucky."

He picks it up. The bug is massive, bigger than I first thought when looking at it. The body is at least five inches long, and the wings slap against the side of the mason jar. He peers through the glass. "That is one ugly motherfucker."

"Where are the Feds?"

"On their way. Can you show them out there?"

My irritation sparks, then wanes. I lean over the desk. "What about Tommy and Junior?"

Mason smiles. His skin is grayish but he's still got that spark in his eye. It's what makes me respect him. He works hard, and he loves what he does. He doesn't care about protocol, or who is popular, who is wealthy or connected in this town. "They might get lost," he says. "Do you mind?"

I look at him and he looks at me and I'm right back where I was before the strip club and the cocaine and the breakdown. Like I'm worth something, like there's a tiny bit of hope somewhere. "Not really," I say. "Are you sure?"

"I'm sure."

I nod and head to my office to pick up a map of the town. Brenda is on the phone in the hallway, speaking loudly. My boots squeak as I head down the hall and into my old office. My desk sits there, the wood polished smooth. Some dust lines the lamp but otherwise it looks like it's ready for me.

"Jessica," Brenda calls. "The Feds are here."

I grab the map, shut the door to the office, and head to the front of the room. The sun shines, as always. The day is new and fresh inside this building, while outside, the trees rot, and the stink of decay carries on the wind.

It takes twenty minutes to get from the precinct downtown to James's house. I drive the sheriff's SUV with the three scientists in back. I still have the rifle, even though I know a few bullets is not going to stop a hundred thousand cicadas from prying the flesh off our bones. Still, I keep it close as I park near the edge of the tobacco field and lead them around the line of trees.

The scientists are mostly quiet. There are two men and one woman who leads the way. They have cameras with them and take pictures every couple of seconds. The smell of rot out here is strong. All the trees are covered in sticky, wet cicada piss, and when the woman sticks her knife into the bark and peels it back, the wood is all brown goop.

"They attacked the two people who live here," I say.

"What were their injuries?" the woman asks. The name on her nametag reads Sabina Gonzalez, and while she did introduce herself earlier, I realized halfway through the car ride that I wasn't really listening to any of them.

"Mostly flesh wounds. The wife was knocked over while trying to escape and sprained her wrist in the fall."

Sabina makes a face.

"She's okay. They're staying in the town motel for a while, though."

The sun stretches high over the crops. The sound of the heat undulates as it beats down over the earth. We tromp through the woods in silence, and from the looks on the scientists' faces, I know this is not normal. They take more pictures, some samples from the trees. "You said you had a cicada sample?" Sabina asks.

"Back at the precinct."

She looks down the rows of trees, the nesting bugs, the dead leaves. One of the men walks up next to her. He wears oversized black glasses that might be considered cool or chic on someone younger, but on him they just look nerdy. "Who's to say they're the same kind? We'll need to grab one," he says.

"I wouldn't suggest that."

He turns to look at me. "Why not?"

"Did you not hear what's been happening? There are a hundred thousand of these fuckers in the trees here. If they swarm or get mad, we're fucked."

"Cicadas aren't aggressive."

"These ones are."

We stand there, facing off. Finally, he breaks my gaze and heads over to the other male scientist. The heat wavers around us, broken by a cool breeze from up in the mountains. Sabina touches my hand. "I think we've gotten all we need. Can you drive us back?"

Her skin is warm, smooth. She's probably a little older than Natasha and married. I spotted the ring on her finger before I even knew her name. I never used to do that, and I'm not sure why I do it now. Lena wasn't married. Natasha isn't, either.

I motion to the two men that we're heading back. They nod and begin picking up their cameras and samples. I turn and start my way back through the brown and wilting tobacco leaves. "It makes me sad," I say.

"What does?"

"The crops. They used to be so beautiful this time of year."

We plod through a maze of dead things. They stretch for an acre, rows and rows of brown before a ledge of acacias and the curve of the springs. A single scarecrow stands, stark, over the field. Finally, we make it to the SUV, but only one of the men is behind us. Glasses isn't there.

"Where's the other guy?" I ask him.

"Who, Johannes? He said he was getting a sample."

"What kind of sample?"

He looks at me like I'm the stupidest person in the fucking universe. "One of the cicadas, of course."

Of course.

Tension seizes my gut. I flush hot. "Get in the SUV and shut the doors," I tell them.

Sabina eyes me. "What is it?"

"Just get in the fucking car."

The two of them obey, and then I'm tromping back through the dead tobacco leaves again, my boots stomping into their decay. On the horizon, a smudge of dark cloud threatens. Rain. It spreads across the blue sky. I walk faster.

Glasses stands at the edge of the trees, at one closest to the line of dead tobacco plants. He has a mesh scooper in his hand and waves it around at the cicadas at the lowest rung of tree. "Stop," I call to him.

He waves me away.

"Put that down!"

He reaches. The bottom of the mesh net scrapes the mass of cicadas. For a second, everything is quiet. Then the humming sound begins. A thousand wings flutter in the bright light of the morning. Glasses drops the net. Takes a step back.

The bugs descend. It happens so quickly, I almost can't react. They drop in a disorganized mass—not just the group from that one tree, but all of them. Tree after tree after tree. It's like a tornado of bugs. The sound vibrates.

I bring the rifle up and fire three shots into the air. The swarm dissipates enough that I'm able to run forward, grab Glasses by the wrist, and drag him back to the SUV with me. The bugs

sting at my skin, dropping and stinging, dropping and stinging. Pain branches through my arms and hands. I keep moving
forward, my free arm shielding my face. Finally, we make it to
the car, and I yank open the back door, shoving Glasses inside.
Swatting, I make it to the driver's seat. A few of the cicadas slip
in with me and there's a moment where all four of us are swatting and yelling until they've all been smashed by specimen
jars, and flashlight butts, and boots.

When it all quiets down, I check the rearview mirror. Glasses
is bleeding on his face in several areas. The wounds look like
small bites where the skin has been punctured. I have a few
spots along my arms and hands. The disorganized swarm bangs
against the glass of the car windshield for a little longer before
meandering away.

"Everyone okay?" I ask. The sound of labored breathing fills
the car. "I've got a first aid kit if anyone needs it."

Silence. Then, Sabina turns to me. "This is what you've been
dealing with?"

Her eyes are wild. A smashed cicada lies on the dash in front
of her, one of its wings still fluttering, a refraction of light making it look rainbow colored, like a bubble. I shrug. "I've never
been stung before."

"That's not normal."

"That's why you're here." I take the sample jar from next to
her and scoop the cicada on the dash into it. "And now you've
got your specimen."

EIGHT

GLASSES AND THE OTHER MAN RETURN TO DC with the specimen to run tests as quickly as possible. I wait with Sabina as she clicks through her computer files with her colleague on speakerphone. The sun is at its strongest now—near 2:00 p.m., but the clouds are closing in. They roll, black and circular, and the distant sound of thunder threatens. Brenda bandaged up my wounds with small, circular Band-Aids. Sabina took a blood sample, but I doubt there will be anything strange in the results. James and his wife are fine, and it's been days.

"Jessica," Mason calls. He sits at the comm desk, holding a file folder in his hands, and I head over to him. At this point, we're pretty useless. Fish and Wildlife will handle the rest. Our part is played, if we ever had one at all. "The mayor wants a presentation at the council meeting at two thirty."

"Awesome. What do you need from me?"

Mason slaps the file folder down on the table. "You're going."

"What? Why?"

"Docs told me to stay off the leg. That means you're traveling."

I lean against the desk and cross my arms. "I just got my blood sucked by seventeen-year-old cicadas."

"You'll survive."

It feels like a test, though I don't know for what. I look down at his leg. The ankle is still incredibly swollen. The flesh pulses red and pink, pressing out from the inside. He has hairy ankles. An old army tattoo peeks out from beneath the hem of his uniform.

I open my mouth to complain again when I think about Natasha. Maybe this is the reason she's acting so strange. Maybe the job and the work I'm doing is finally making her look at me differently. Maybe I'm finally someone to her, and she doesn't know how to deal with it. "I have fifteen minutes until I need to leave," I say. "What would you like me to say to them?"

🐜

My stomach is tight as I make my way up the steps to the council meeting room. In college and high school, I avoided public speaking as much as possible. That's why I never became a politician—that and too much ass-kissing. I figured being a cop was as good a way as any to help people, and I wouldn't really have to deal with crowds too much.

Now, even though I've addressed them before, I'm acutely aware of the fact that Natasha will be in the room, too.

I wipe my palms on my pants. My hands are pocked with Band-Aids. My uniform pulls taut over my chest and arms. Besides the stupid Band-Aids, I look smart. The blue coloring in the uniform goes well with my fair hair and I've developed a light tan from being outside so much.

Taking a breath, I open the door to the council room. The smell of dust and velvet jumps out at me. Everyone sits around an oval wood table in suits and business casual, wrinkled faces, gray skin, frowns. Wedding rings. "Thanks for inviting me," I say.

I scan the room. Old white guy, old white guy, old white guy. My eyes finally land on Natasha. She's seated near the middle of the table on the left-hand side. She wears a white collared shirt with the top two buttons undone, and a long silver necklace rests over her breasts. Her pants are high-waisted, pulling at her hips. Her eyes rest on the papers sitting in front of her.

The mayor motions at me and I make my way over to him. He's a short, fat man with a balding crown of hair who smells like moth balls and fresh dollar bills. "Mason told me he was injured," he says.

"He's recovering. But it's hard for him to get around."

He looks slightly inconvenienced in that way all white men look when they have to deal with someone who's not another white man. I smile. Sit down in the chair next to him. It's cushioned, slick with velvet. My palms sweat. I place them face down on the table and the wood is cool to the touch. "So, talk to us about what's going on, and what you're doing to fix this problem," he says.

I shift. My clothes make a stiff sound. Natasha glances up at me and her eyes meet mine. She holds, strong and sure. She's not looking at me how I want. It's not with desire, or envy. It's this soft, babying look, this thing that makes me feel like a fifteen-year-old kid in overalls all over again, instead of the lead investigator on this case. My cheeks heat. "I'm going to be honest with you. We don't know exactly why it's happening yet, but we've got about a hundred thousand cicadas on the Monongahela tree line near James's property. They like to swarm and bite if disturbed." I hold up my hand and peel off one of the Band-Aids, revealing a pinkish red hole in my skin. The council breaks into grunts and whispers.

"Fish and Wildlife is examining some samples now to see what's going on."

"We have a crisis, then," the mayor says.

"Stay away from the line. Don't fool with any of the bugs if you see them. Same old, same old. This happened because a scientist bothered the swarm. If he hadn't, we'd be fine."

The mayor stares at me. His eyes are lined with red veins. I've never noticed how tired he looks, probably because I've never really looked at him up close before. He's not an ugly man, but he is void. I look in his face and I see something blank, the same blank thing I've noticed in Natasha when she doesn't need to see me. I wish I could be like them, blocking things out when they are inconvenient, when they hurt. "And what are you doing to fix the problem?"

"The next step is extermination, if possible."

"If possible?"

"We want to do as little harm to the forest as possible."

Outside, the clouds have rolled in and rain starts to splash against the windows. I can hear the wind, the distant boom of thunder. Storms here are long and devastating. They roll through one, two at a time. Lightning catches the barns on fire and knocks out power lines.

"Any questions?" I ask.

"There's got to be more we can do," the mayor says.

"You have to let us ride it out."

"I don't believe this," one of the council members says. "Mason should be here."

My cheeks heat. In the middle of the ceiling, a dangly chandelier spreads light over the table. I can feel it on my face, warming. "Mason is doing his job. And last time I checked, no one is this room was qualified to make decisions for him."

All I can hear is my own breathing and the breathing of the mayor, somewhat labored. I stand. My chest is heavy. I've worked so hard to be here, to get opportunities, to be respected, and no one in this room is ever really going to look at me. Natasha is never going to see me, no matter how good of a fuck I am, or what kind of work I'm doing. In her mind, I'll always be that fifteen-year-old girl in overalls, trying vodka for the first time and doing her makeup.

"Follow the rules we've already set in place and you'll all be fine. We'll let you know when the situation's been handled."

My boots creak the old floor as I head for the exit. A painting of man in a wig and red robes stares out at me from a portrait on the wall. From behind me, I can feel the gazes of the council as I walk out the door.

❧

I'm almost to the metal detectors when the stalk of heeled wedges fills the hallway. I'm still fuming but a part of me feels this intense wave of pleasure as she grabs my wrist and turns me so we're face to face. We're out in the open, in front of a group of teenagers. Her curls are tighter than normal, like she did her hair in a rush this morning, and she's got on lipstick, which she normally doesn't wear. It's soft pink. A good color for the paleness of her skin.

"Come to my office," she says. She has that intense look she gets when she's in the middle of a project. Her eyes are wide, and her lips are parted slightly.

"Why?"

"I need to talk to you."

"Really?"

"Please."

Students pass around us, chattering, wearing their little school uniforms, taking pictures with their phones. I wonder why the fuck they are so excited. This place is nothing like they describe it in school. This is a place where people talk around things. They usher in their friends, follow the party line, and nothing ever changes.

"Jess," Natasha says. "Come on."

After a few seconds, I relent and follow her down the hall to her office. She still hasn't cleaned—papers line her desk, not even in piles but fanned out. A nip of vodka rests next to her laptop. One of her framed posters has broken in the corner and sits crookedly next to the window. It's faintly scented of her perfume, and I have the momentary urge to pull her into my chest and smell her neck.

"You got hurt?" she asks.

Rain slathers the window. The droplets are large and fat and mist has rolled in so thick, I can't even see out the window. It must be the biggest storm we've had this summer. "I'm fine."

"Look at your hands."

"They weren't covered by the uniform," I say. "This damn thing is so starchy. The rest of it covered me good."

She stands, one arm on her desk, tilted so she's shorter than me. Her eyes scan across the wounds, squinting. "I hate to see you hurt."

I stick my hands in my pockets. "I'm fine."

Her hair coils tight. I wonder why she's chosen to wear lipstick today, and if she's doing it because she knows Mark will be around, if they have secret rendezvous throughout the day here. The thought of it makes me so mad, I can barely breathe. "This problem is getting worse," she says.

"Every problem gets worse before it gets better."

She makes a face. "Mark ran an editorial this morning. You should keep him posted."

"That's not my job. He can reach out to me."

Her head cocks to the side. "Are you giving me attitude?"

"What the fuck else would I be doing?"

We stare at one another and after a while, a smile crosses her face, small and mischievous. And goddamn if it doesn't get me. A smirk tugs at my mouth. I try to stifle it, but it spreads quick and easy. Her smile always does me in. I could be on death row, look up and see her smiling at me with the death needle in her hand, and I'd smile back.

I hesitate before pulling her into a hug. She rests her chin on my shoulder. Her body is warm. I want to do more, something to make her love me, but I'm not sure what would work. "Do you have a long day?" I ask into her hair. She breathes against my neck, sending goosebumps across my skin. When I go to pull back, she keeps me there. Her palms warm my back.

"Every day is long," she says.

Wind howls. A slip of lightning lights the window, then disappears. The world is dark and blue colored, tinted with the brief flashes of storm. *You win some, you lose some*, my dad would say. But it feels like I'm always losing.

※

The storm worsens. By 5:00 p.m., the county is under a tornado watch, and rain batters the street, sending sluices of runoff down the concrete and into the gutters. The sky turns pitch-black. I haven't seen it like this in years, since I was a child. Mason and I put Sabina up in the local hotel with a tornado shelter and give her a walkie in case the power or cell service drops out. Her coworkers are back in DC by now, their samples in the lab being tested. "It won't be long," she says.

I go home, even though Mason asks me to stay at the precinct. It's a concrete bunker, basically, and my cabin is more like a shack. But I've worked hard over the past year to clean it up, make it look nice, and I'll be damned if some storm is going to tear it apart without me in it.

Driving home, the roads flood with water. That's the problem with living in the valley—all the rain pours down the mountains and then has nowhere to go. The swamp fills. The drains fill. And then we sit in it for weeks.

I slow over a large puddle in the road, then start rising in altitude. For flooding, the cabin is ideally located. It's at a rise in the hill, on the way out of town. The school buses would never come out here, but we never got flooded out, either.

The turn onto my driveway is blocked by a downed tree branch, so I roll to a stop and get out to move it. Thunder crashes overhead. Lightning purples the trees, casting a gray sheen over the land before dissipating. I have this pain in my chest, right under my breast. It stabs into me as rain wets my hair, slicking down my uniform.

My body immediately grows chilled. I drag the branch across the driveway and shove it off into the corner. Another crash of thunder and then a blue-green flash illuminates the sky in the distance—a power line down.

I hurry back to the car and hop in, soaked. Water runs down my forehead in streams. Visibility drops as I make my way down the driveway, the gravel kicking up under the undercarriage in mucky gobs.

As soon as I open the door to the house, I'm hit with a wave of warm air that's collected throughout the day. I open one of the windows a crack to let the cooler air in, grab a beer, and get busy moving the furniture away from the rest of the windows.

It's really not that bad being out here during the storm. Being alone is what I know. I've done it most of my life. Both my parents worked. Meg was off at college before I started high school and I never had girlfriends, not even in college. There was no one until Lena, and I'm starting to think there might not be anyone after her, either.

A boom of thunder shakes the house. I'm turning to grab an emergency kit, some food, and drinks, when I spot something on the other side of the kitchen. Peering closer, my stomach cramps up. It's a cicada. "Fucker."

My immediate instinct is to smash it to death with my boots but I'm in socked feet, having taken left my shoes at the door. I'm exposed. Vulnerable.

I glance around for something to kill it with. The puncture wounds on my hands are hurting now, the adrenaline of the morning having finally worn off, and seeing one of those things up close sends a jolt through them.

There's an old phone book on the kitchen counter. I grab it and move closer. I've almost reached the bug when it notices me and scuttles to the wall. I chase after it, but the thing moves quickly, scampering across the wood floor, up the wall, and to the open window. The ledge is wet with rain. Droplets stain the floor.

The cicada climbs into the night and I slam the windowpane shut after it.

I peer out, trying to see where the little fucker came from. A giant oak tree stands next to the house. It was always a danger growing up—the long branches could easily crush the side of the house—but my parents never had enough money to get it removed safely. Somehow, after all these years, it's still standing.

I squint and spot something moving over the tree. It's impossible to see clearly in the darkness, so I grab a flashlight from one of the kitchen drawers and shine it out into the night. At first, I don't know what I'm looking at. Then, I spot the black, liquored shell of the wings, sleek in the reflection of the flashlight. Thousands of the bugs flutter, hiving over the tree. I drop the flashlight.

I pull the curtains over the window and grab the walkie. "Mason?"

Static. I wonder if his walkie has run out of battery. Then it fizzles out and his voice echoes through the line. "I hear ya, Jess."

"They're here."

"Who's here?"

"The bugs. They're swarming over the oak tree out at my place."

Static crackles. Pain echoes in my chest again and I touch the spot there with two fingers. "Must've migrated in the storm," Mason says. "I wouldn't worry."

"They're swarming, Mason."

The walkie is silent for a few beats, then he says, "You know what to do. Stay inside. Stay locked up."

I close my eyes, lean back against the wall. Force my breathing to slow. I can feel the storm through the house, the rattle of thunder, the static in the air. I wonder then what it felt like for my mom and dad and Meg in the car that night they crashed. It was raining, a downpour like this one, I was told. I imagine them on the old highway in the early morning light, the headlights cutting across the darkened roadway.

The tires hit a wet spot. The car slid before hitting the telephone pole, and the force wrapped the small SUV around metal and wood. Meg was in the backseat. Although she survived the original hit, she died from the swelling in her brain in the hospital. I was still trying to get there when she passed. It seemed especially cruel, to have that hope for a moment that she would pull through, and then to see it fade again just as quickly.

I lose power for about four hours. The house shudders and shakes. I hole up in the downstairs closet, just under the stairs, and sit with my emergency pack and flashlight, some power bars and a six-pack. I burn through the first three beers quickly, then start to get buzzed and slow down.

It's never more clear how alone you are than when you're camped out in the closet under the stairs during a tornado and town-wide crisis. I look down at my phone; no cell service. I flick the walkie on and off, on and off. I drink another beer, then another. There are some games in here, and some old books. I take them off the shelves and peer through them.

Meg and I used to play Scrabble a lot when she was in college and I was in high school. It was fun for her but for me, it was a competition. I played to see if I could beat her, and I did, often. She coined words like, *dance, grass, play.* I coined words like *superstition, molecule, moat.* She never cared when she lost, while to me, life was all about winning and losing. I lost every day when I went to school, when a girl I wanted to be friends with stuck gum in my hair, to the time I got ratted out for pushing a girl that bullied me off the monkey bars.

"She got what was coming to her," I told the principal. I was in the fourth grade and they suspended me for a month. The bully kept on beating everyone else up, and when I returned, she lied and told everyone I'd tried to touch her between her legs. That's why I'd pushed her, she said. Because I was mad she wouldn't let me.

I stopped being near girls after that and stopped sticking up for myself. When I realized I was gay, I tried to hide it. I hated myself for it. I was gross. I was weird. I was a predator. *I hurt someone*, I thought. No one was ever going to want me. But then there was Natasha, sitting across from me at the dinner table in high school, that stupid, beautiful smile on her lips. I watched her pick at pepperoni pizza, wipe her lips with a napkin, sip wine. I watched her tilt back her head when Meg cracked jokes, her laughter short, loud, staccato, filling the room.

I realized I loved Natasha one night at the house after the crash. She was helping me clean up the bottom floor. It was covered in dirt and dust. I'd spent the whole week selling and moving furniture around and scuff marks marred the wood floors. She stood in jeans. I watched her as she moved around the room. She didn't have that bell shape to her waist like Lena did, but her hips tapered in a way that drew my eye.

"What else has to go?" she asked.

I looked around the room. It was just the couch and coffee

table, which I wanted to keep. The old rocker would have to be trashed, and then there was the bookshelf Natasha stood next to. My chest panged looking at it. "We can get rid of the rocker."

"You want to put it outside? I'll get someone to junk it for you."

"I got it, Nat."

She looked around the room. Her hand settled on the bookshelf. "And this?"

I hesitated. "The bookshelf was Meg's. Dad made it for her."

Natasha removed her hand. Her entire face tightened in a way I hadn't seen before, and after a moment, she went back to sweeping. It was quiet inside, the sound of the woods dulled by the soft hush of the central air. I waited, but Natasha didn't say anything. The broom scraped the floor in a rhythmic pattern.

"I'd feel weird getting rid of it, but I don't want to look at it, either."

Natasha kept moving. She was a good worker, at least with the broom. She broomed that fucking room like her life depended on it. Sweat pasted along her brow as I glanced up at her. She looked lost in thought. Her brow was knit. Then her lips scrunched up and she stopped sweeping. She held the broom vertical as her eyes clouded. Her mouth pinched.

"Do you want it?" I asked. "She loved that thing."

Natasha exhaled, then started to cry.

It felt like someone had killed me watching her dissolve like that. Her face wrinkled, and the sorrow poured out of her. I stiffened, put down the rag in my hand and wiped my palms on my jeans. "Nat?"

She turned away from me, resting the broom against the wall and heading for one of the windows. I followed. My heart raced. I couldn't figure out what to do, comfort her or pretend it wasn't happening. I felt like I should pretend it wasn't happening; she had never cried in front of me before. But then I heard her breath, a sharp inhalation, and I was done for. I moved forward, wrapping my arms around her waist. It was the first time I'd really touched her. The hug at the funeral didn't count. It was compulsory, and her arms left mine after a mere second of holding. This was different. I let my hands rest over her belly. She was warm and solid, stronger than I expected.

"I'm sorry," I said.

She stayed there for a little, not saying anything. My arms held tight around her body. She exhaled, and the crying slowed. She pulled herself together through breath and muscle, then quieted. I let go. When she turned around, she mustered a smile. "Don't be sorry," she said. She looked so different. Her eyes were sad in a way she hadn't yet allowed them to be around me, and it made her breathtaking.

"Are you okay?"

She forced another smile and her hands sought mine out. Her palms were warm, dry. "Let's finish up," she said.

She went back to normal almost immediately, but I couldn't stop thinking about it, even days after. It was like she'd gotten lodged inside me that afternoon, and I couldn't get rid of her. A week later, I started thinking about what it would be like to take her to bed. I started wondering what it would be like to wake up to her in the morning. If her hair would flatten on the side she slept on, and if she'd stay in bed later than me, and expect coffee in the morning. I pictured us old together, and her running for office somewhere. I wanted us together in a way that hurt in my bones.

🐜

The storm ends eventually. The house stops shaking and the noises outside cease. I'm good and drunk by then and crawl out of the closet space under the stairs on my hands and knees. I move to the window and look out into the night. My phone says it's 1:00 a.m., but I have no service.

Four days until the anniversary now.

I peer out into the darkness. Some tree branches have fallen in the yard. Small pieces of wood, halved and broken, muck the grass. Otherwise, not much seems to have happened. The house sounds intact, at least from here. After lying on the wood floor for a while, I go to the window where the cicada was and check the old oak tree. My head spins as I shine a light into the night.

There's nothing there so I figure the storm must've scared them away. I wonder if they're gone from the rest of the town or if they've lingered, hunkered down under the thick pine leaves and branches.

After a while, I decide to go to bed, but not before checking my phone again for service. There's nothing. I pull up my text thread with Natasha. The last thing she wrote me was, *Are you coming or no?*

I enter the text box. Write, *I love you, you know.* Send the text.

Then I clamber upstairs, kicking my socks off at the top. I pad down the hall, pausing for a moment at Meg's room before passing by it. I grab the pillow that Natasha used the other night and return to Meg's old bed. The sheets are starchy, unused. I bring the pillow to my chest and breathe in, trying to catch Natasha's scent, but it just smells like pine from the house. My eyes close.

I think about how it is to sleep forever, and to not have to face the sun or the night or anything in between. I think about how quiet it must be, and good. It must be nice for dead people. Moving from place to place. Never held down. I wonder if it's beautiful, or if it's just darkness and nothing, for the rest of forever.

NINE

IN THE MORNING, THE WORLD SEEMS BRIGHTER. The sun shines in, burning through the windows. I wake up in the middle of the bed, sprawled sideways with the covers on the floor. This is usually how I wake up when I'm alone. I thrash in the night. The only times I stayed still were when Natasha slept over, or on the rare nights Lena let me stay with her. Those times, I slept like a log. No movement. I'd pass out on my side and was dead to the world for hours.

I yawn. My mouth is dry. I sit up and feel immediately like shit. After twenty-six, my hangovers started becoming a problem, and now at thirty, every part of me aches with them. I check my phone after heading downstairs; there's service again, and my drunken text to Natasha has gone through with no response.

Great.

I toss my phone onto the sofa. There's nothing worse than loving someone who doesn't love you back. It's like loving someone who has died, except sometimes you have to see them in public and acknowledge how they don't love you back.

I head upstairs. The power is back on, so I take a shower and clean myself up. Then I decide to make breakfast. I used to be okay at it. I whipped up omelets and hash browns and ham fried with egg yolk and paprika. I poured my parents Bloody Marys and dusted their bananas foster with powdered sugar. They asked for breakfasts on the weekends, and whenever one of them was mad at me, I'd make them French toast and then life was good again.

After lingering in the bathroom for a while, I head downstairs and put some potatoes on the grill. Then I add bacon strips, butter, eggs, and asparagus. It's too early for asparagus but it smells good, and after a while, the tissue softens. I smother it with cheese sauce and look at my masterpiece like I am a fucking genius.

Still no text from Natasha.

The walkie squawks. I startle in my seat, then turn to pick it up off the empty chair next to me. "Make it through the night?" Mason asks.

I chew. "More or less. Bad damage in town?"

"Can you help clean up?"

"Give me half an hour."

Static. Then, "You sure you're okay?"

My eggs are a bit runny and the yolk smears into the asparagus and cheese sauce. I've never learned the line with making eggs. Either they're too runny or I put them on too long and they go green or burn. I can never quite get that in-between. "You better fucking hire me back after all this," I say.

"Yeah, yeah."

I put the walkie down on the table and stab at my bacon. Grease lingers on the plate. I finish eating and clean up quickly, then head outside. Tree branches lie splintered and broken across the yard. Many of the leaves have been ripped off the branches, plastering the sides of my car and house. Pockets of water line the driveway. It's impassible, even with my SUV.

After spending twenty minutes clearing the driveway, I finally head downtown. The road has already been cleared by the state, but I still take it slow, looking for signs of the bugs. They weren't anywhere near the house this morning. I couldn't hear their hum or see any signs of their damage on the tree, but part of me has this feeling that they're still around somewhere, hiding.

My thoughts move to Natasha. I wonder if she lost power, too. If the apartment building is still in good shape. Suddenly, I'm gripped with fear that something's happened to her. She usually texts back, no matter what. I think about stopping by her apartment but I'm already late getting to town, so I tell myself she's fine. She's probably holed up somewhere with Mark.

I approach the town and several trees are down. The swing set is down, too. One of the poles supporting it lies at an angle, jutting out into the sky. Mason limps around the edge of the park with Tommy and Junior, his sheriff's hat pulled down over his ears. I park at the curb and head over to them. "I thought you were supposed to be resting," I say.

He turns to look at me and his skin is ashen. The wrinkles around his eyes are like mountain folds.

"God, you look like shit."

He glares. "Glad you survived the night."

"Seen any bugs today?"

"Not so far. Storm maybe scared them off."

I glance around. Most of the buildings look like they have power. The lights are on in the town hall and I bet my life Natasha is in there already, working. The sun shines. It's a warm day, with less humidity now that the storm has passed, but I still work up a sweat clearing the debris.

We finish by midday and retire to the precinct where Brenda has Sabina set up in my old office. After showering, I seek her out. She hunches over the computer, squinting. Dark shadows rim her eyes. I take a seat on the desk where she works. My neck is wet from the shower still, moisture curling into my collar.

"Find out anything yet?"

She doesn't look up. "The tests found elevated hormone levels."

"So, they're horny?"

She laughs. "It's probably more complicated than that."

I stand there, waiting for her to elaborate, but she never does. "How do we stop them from hurting people?"

A shrug. "Stay away from them."

I rise. The door is open to the hallway and the sound of Brenda's voice on the comm system filters through. Shadows stretch from the open door, like a rising black cloud. It still smells like dust in here, but it's been tinted by Sabina's perfume, something clean and strong, like Natasha's. "I don't like that answer," I say.

Sabina looks up from the computer. She really is a good-looking woman. Her eyebrows are thick, eyes dark. Her skin has no blemishes. "We hesitate to destroy them all. Surely you understand."

"They're dangerous. And they're hurting the town, the trees. You've seen it."

"Everything will regrow."

"People's livelihoods have been destroyed. Those crops won't be viable until next year."

Sabina shifts, rapping her knuckles against the desk twice before standing. She's tall, taller than me. I wonder what her husband looks like, and if he's taller than her. If he's handsome. I bet he is. Women like her always end up with tall, handsome men with good jobs. "It's not really up to either of us," she says. "The USDA will decide." She shuts her laptop and starts shoving it into a black briefcase. The sun falls in strips around her. "We'll work on a stunning agent and then we can redistribute the population."

"Redistribute them?"

"Separate and relocate them somewhere safe."

I watch her zip up the briefcase, her slim fingers moving over the pockets. "But what if they come back? What if the same thing happens again next year?"

"Magicicadas only emerge every seventeen years."

"But what about the regular cicadas? What's to say there's not something in the forest making them act like that? Some bacteria or something?"

Her lips purse. She brings her eyes to mine. "You know, I never got a chance to say it, but thank you for what you did back there."

"Don't change the subject."

She smiles. "I mean at the farm. Helping Johannes."

Heat flushes my cheeks. I think back to the stupid man with the glasses and how he almost got all of us killed. I think about next year, and how, if this happens again, I will never let anyone fuck with the swarm. No matter how smart they think they are. "Don't thank me. I should've stopped him from even trying."

Sabina lifts the strap of the briefcase to her shoulder, rounding the desk to stand in front of me. Our eyes meet. I can smell her perfume. "You're hard on yourself," she says. "But you're good at your job."

She touches my shoulder and for a moment, a well of emotion surfaces inside me. I feel like I'm going to cry. She squeezes, and then the warmth of her hand is gone, and the room feels cold, even with the strip of sun warming the wood tile.

The idea of a stunning agent and relocation of the bugs goes up in front of the council. I'm called to testify about it, along with Mason and Sabina. She arranges to call in while heading back to DC. Mason brings me to the diner for lunch before we're scheduled to speak. We sit in the same booth I sat with Natasha only a few days earlier.

He orders food like I do: eggs, bacon, toast with jam. He slices butter and puts it in his grits, then gives me a funny look when I ask for cheese with mine. "God made cheese to go with grits," I say, when he catches my eye.

"Grits and butter," he grunts. "That's the only way."

We sit, knives over plates. Most of the dead trees fell during the storm and now only the healthy ones survive. They leave gaps along the promenade, the central park. We've removed the swing set and now the playground looks auspiciously void. "Why did you hire me in the first place?" I ask.

Mason chews, stabs a piece of bacon. "You had experience."

"You knew my reputation here."

"You had good references."

I dump salt and pepper in my grits and stir them together. My mom used to make them with cheddar cheese. There was nothing better, she said. But at the diner, they make them with American. The result is a mesh of white and orange, melted and stringing as I pull my spoon from it.

"What's this about?" Mason asks. He keeps his head down, shoveling the maximum amount of food into his mouth with optimum speed. A smear of grits catches in his mustache. "You upset about something?"

"No."

He chews. Bacon grease idles on the plate, catching the light from the lamp above us. The waitresses bustle back and forth. The smell of toast, faint fire, lingers in the restaurant.

"I don't know why I'm doing this," I say.

"Doing what?"

I take a sip of orange juice. "Living here."

One of the waitresses refills Mason's coffee and I cover my cup when she tries to refill mine. Mason takes four sugars and rips the top off the packets, then dumps them in the dark liquid. He doesn't bother to stir before bringing the cup to his lips and drinking. "You got the house."

"Fuck the house. You know what I mean."

"I don't," he says.

I look down at my plate. It's sad that the only person I have to talk to about my problems is my boss, the person that dragged me raging and screaming out of a strip club, the back pockets of my jeans stuffed with one-dollar bills.

"This about Natasha?"

My cheeks heat. "That obvious, huh?"

"You're not exactly subtle."

I bring the grits to my mouth. They're good but not like my mom's. The chef puts milk in them, which makes them a little too rich for my taste. I put the spoon back. Mash it around.

"I was almost married," Mason says. "Ten years ago."

"Really?"

"There was this other guy . . . she liked him. I didn't push it." He finishes his bacon. "I should've." He finishes his bacon and wipes his mustache with a red cloth napkin. Then he puts his hands flat on the table. His fingers are callused, cracked near the knuckles from sun and hard labor. He is close to fifty and still bare a ring.

"That was stupid of you," I say.

His raises his eyebrows at me and I get his point, but it's different for him. He's a sheriff. People respect him around town. He has enough money that he could probably buy nice things for a wife and take her on cool vacations. He drives a nice car. I've had the same SUV for ten years and have never figured out how to cook eggs correctly.

Testifying in front of the council is like going to the dentist for a root canal. I should really be anesthetized for it, but unfortunately I'm stone cold sober when I walk in the room. It's later in the day by then, close to 4:00 p.m. The council sits around the same table I addressed them at earlier, only this time, Mason is with me. He hobbles in and takes a seat at the head of the table.

I sit next to him. Natasha is only a few seats away from me, but I can't bring myself to look her in the eye.

There's this buzzing energy in the room. The light is dim with the curtains drawn like they are; the air feels a few degrees warmer than normal. It's more like a dinner party than anything else. One where at the end, someone is going to be sacrificed.

From across the table, Sabina's voice echoes through the speakerphone but I don't listen to what she says. It's the same old, same old.

I keep having this ringing in my ears.

Out of habit, I turn to look at Natasha. She's looking at the speakerphone on the other side of the table. From this angle, I observe her profile: small nose, pointed slightly, her hair springing from her head, brushing her chin. She has a nice chin and the skin under her neck is taut. I glance over the freckles that plaster her face. She turns to me and I look away. I can feel her gaze on me for several moments before she goes back to the speakerphone.

"The stunning agent should be effective and will give us an opportunity to remove them safely," Sabina says.

The mayor leans forward. "You know this because you've used it before?"

"Well," Sabina says. "No."

Silence sweeps the room. Through a slip in the curtains, dust rises in a sliver of natural light. "What do you mean, no?" The mayor asks.

"We just haven't used it in the field yet."

"Is it dangerous?"

"Of course not," she says. "Not for humans. It will stun the cicadas. They might fall out of the trees, but it won't kill them."

"But how do you know that it won't do any harm if you've never used it?"

"It's been tested—"

"But we'll be the first group you've ever used it on in the field," I jump in.

The group is silent, faces tilted my way. After a few moments, Sabina clears her throat. I realize then that she was more into this than she let on. She was the boss, she was calling the shots all along. "There is no risk to the town," she says. "I can assure you of that."

The room stays silent for a few moments and then Natasha leans forward in her seat. She has that edged look to her face, and I can tell what's coming before she even opens her mouth. "I'm sorry. Am I not understanding this? We're really considering releasing an untested agent on our forest?"

"It's not untested—" Sabina begins.

"You just said it hasn't been used yet in the field."

Sabina is quiet, and I wonder if she has ever faced someone like Natasha before, someone who gives zero fucks about anything you have to say after she's formed an opinion and will refuse to be swayed or placated unless some tiny part of her somewhere agrees to listen. "A completely untested agent is different from one that hasn't been used in the field. Our tests show no dangerous side effects."

"But if you haven't used them here, what's to say they won't interact with our environment badly?" Natasha looks around the table. "We're not seriously considering this. Are we?"

By the lack of assent, it's clear we are. The council leans back in their chairs, crossing and uncrossing their arms. The room is quiet, brimming with that same kind of energy that surfaces before a big movement. Like the electricity I felt before the cicadas attacked us in the field.

The council looks at each other. Finally, the mayor speaks up. "We can't sit here and do nothing. This is our only option." A chorus of mumblings and nods. "All in favor of releasing this stunning agent, say aye."

A union of voices answers.

"Nays?"

Only Natasha and the oldest council member, Johnny, speak up. A beat passes before the mayor folds his hands on the table and says, "I believe the ayes have it."

"Mayor—" Natasha begins.

"Councilwoman, the group has spoken."

Her eyes light with fire, the eyes I love. Then she looks away from the table and starts collecting her things.

After the meeting disperses, I track her through the building to the break room, where there's a small vending and Keurig machine. She slips a new K-cup in it, then takes an apple out from the fridge. Toward the end of the day, she's always eating apples. I used to hear her crunching on them from down the hall before I started working the entrance. Like clockwork.

There is so much about Natasha that is predictable. Whenever she'd leave her office for a meeting and say, "This won't take very long," I knew I wouldn't see her for the rest of the day. On Tuesday nights, she stayed later than usual, and in the winter, she'd always leave her boots at the entrance of the hall, so she could slip into heels before anyone saw her.

I place my hand on the side of the doorframe. "So, are you going to ignore me or what?"

She startles. "Jess."

"I'd really like to talk to you."

The Keurig machine spits out a single cup of coffee for her. The smell of it fills the room. It's plain. She never drinks fun coffee like hazelnut or chocolate macadamia, the flavors I keep in my kitchen. Her drinks are always black. Espresso. Things that are bitter and difficult to stomach. "I know," she says. "We should, but not here."

I cross the room, passing by her. She's stands an inch taller than me today, in heeled wedges. I love them. I love how they look on her. I pick up the cup of coffee that's brewed. "Let's go to your office."

"I was thinking we could wait until I get off."

"You won't leave if I agree to that."

She lets out a sigh. Her eyes are downcast, like they get when she's upset about a work thing. She doesn't smile. "Fine." She takes another bite of the apple and makes her way back through the doorframe. I follow, the coffee quivering in my hand, down the hallway and into the corner office.

It looks like it always looks. She says she's been going to clean it up for months, but it's starting to get to the point where I know she never will. "Did you have any damage from the storm?" I ask. "Looks like your office got hit pretty hard."

She makes a sniffling noise, and when she turns, she's got a small smile on her face. "I'll clean it up soon."

"I'm not really worried about your office."

I place the coffee on her desk. She sets the apple down on top of some papers, half-bitten into with tiny teeth marks creasing its body. Then she sits at her chair and looks up at me, a small smirk twisting her features. "So," she says. "You love me."

"It's not a joke."

"I know." Still, a smile threatens on her lips. She rests her elbow on the desk and plays with her hair. "I'm not making it a joke."

"You're smiling."

"You are, too," she shoots back, and immediately the muscles in my face tense. I didn't even realize I was smiling. Around her, it's impossible not to smile. "Did the house fare okay last night?"

I shift my weight from one leg to another. "It's fine. A bunch of bugs swarmed the oak tree, though."

Her mouth tightens. "Are they still there? Want me to help you get rid of them?"

"No," I fluster, a blush starting in my neck. "I mean, they were gone in the morning."

I can feel her gaze on me, trailing the heat of red that's now setting my neck on fire. I don't know why I'm like this with her. I've had crushes on other women before, but I never got like this with them. At first, I thought it was because she was something special. But now, more and more, I think it's just bad luck. "I'm glad," she says. "You think our problem is solved?"

I shake my head. "We don't know why they showed up."

"So?"

"So that means it could happen again."

She brings the coffee to her lips. It steams around her mouth. She sips. "You're always thinking ten months in advance, aren't you, Rockstar?"

I stare down at her. She really is so beautiful sometimes. She gets this shine about her face, and then with her smile, she becomes this woman you can't look away from. I think maybe she would appear pretty in an ordinary way, if not for the mischievous quirk of her mouth, and the way her eyes light up when she looks at you. "So, that's it?" I ask.

"What else?" she asks. "Tell me what else."

"Nat, come on."

She sighs, turning away from me so she's facing her computer monitor. "I have a lot of work to do, and I can't really deal with this now."

"You always say that."

"Because I apparently can't handle anything anymore." She turns the monitor on and plugs it in to her laptop. The quirk in her mouth is gone now. I look down at what she's wearing—

black sweater with a black pencil skirt and mustard yellow shirt with ruffles. It would look ridiculous on anyone else besides her, but she has this stalwart confidence that makes it all fall together.

"I want us to date," I say. Heat boils in my cheeks, but I stand my ground. "I want to take you places and be your girlfriend."

"Yeah. I figured that." She looks devastated and for a moment I feel like I should probably go kill myself. Then she turns. She looks up and meets my eyes. The happy go lucky look is gone. She's not smiling. "I can't do that, Jess." She looks like she's going to cry. "I'm with Mark."

My throat tightens. I want to laugh but I can't. Overhead, the central air comes on, releasing a slow hiss of sound into the room. It hums in time with the slurred beat of my heart.

"Are you okay?" She reaches out to touch me, but I pull away. The air in the room has gone tart, puckering against us.

"It's fine. I understand."

She grabs at my hand. My body stiffens and I tug away from her, like she did with me then. "Stop," she says. "It doesn't have to be like this."

"How else is it supposed to be?"

She stares at me for a moment. Then her hand falls. Her eyebrows raise. She gets that incredulous look on her face that she gets when she's really, really mad. She's never done this to me before. I've seen it a million times elsewhere, but this is the first time it's been reserved especially for me.

I turn and walk out.

TEN

I TAKE AN OVERNIGHT SHIFT at the precinct to keep myself from thinking too much. Plus, I figure it might be helpful. Mason is exhausted. I can see it in his face. His eyes are glossy, his skin gray. He looks like a statue as Tweedledee and Tweedledum load him up in a car and drive him off to his fancy house only a mile away from Natasha's fancy apartment building. Brenda leaves me with a dish of chicken casserole and I sit at the comm desk eating and chasing it with an ice-cold Coca-Cola. I swig the soda around in my mouth before swallowing, then place the dirty Tupperware in the bathroom sink.

The precinct is silent, dark. I haven't seen any bugs all day, but the smell of dead trees is everywhere, made heavier by the recent rains and stagnant water that puddles along the streets. There's a smell in the precinct, too. I'm not sure what it is. Something stale.

Locked up inside, I watch the bugs peter in and out of the lamplight above the front door. Grasshoppers, moths. A few cicadas land on the glass door. Their bodies bang at the glass, like the one that landed at Natasha's. I peer closely at them, at their multi-colored torsos, their delicate wings. They just sit there, shuffling like little robot bugs, until I open the door and slam it again. The dust clears. They're gone.

For an hour after that, I search the web for information on hormone-driven cicadas, but find nothing. It makes me think

Sabina is lying, that there's something more going on, she just won't tell us.

The shift passes inch by inch, second by second. I clean up the holding cell, mopping the floor and bleaching the sink. The comms are on but no one calls in. The phone sits silent. When I'm finished, I head back to Mason's office and pull out the old radio he's got there. It's coated in dust and hasn't worked since the eighties. But I'm pretty sure it once belonged to his father, so there's no way in hell he's ever going to throw it out.

I tinker around with the wires in the back and eventually get it to turn on, but no stations come through. It's just static and buzzing, and some weird interference that sounds like whales singing. I turn it off and stick it on his desk. He's got his sheriff's academy training certificate there, a picture of him riding a bull at a rodeo in Tennessee. He told me the story once. He stayed on for ten seconds. That's two seconds longer than is required for qualification, and in the end, he won the competition for style. He was twenty-five then.

When I worked here, my office was covered in awards. I had my diploma on one wall, my honors award on the other, and then my DC's Unsung Hero certificate on the filing cabinet. I was so proud of the good grades I got in college, and the way I served the city when I walked the beat.

I try to imagine putting those things up again if I were to move back into the office, but I can't. There's just no reason for it anymore. I put myself through school, made honors, won awards locally for my work, and all for what? I'm still back here in my hometown, in love with a girl who is never going to love me back. Still living alone. I can't imagine ever going back to that person I used to be—the one that was always smiling in pictures and looked forward to a life I thought would be good because I'd earned it.

After another hour, I get bored and decide to go for a drive. I circle around the block a few times, then head deeper into the woods, where the bulk of the houses are. The night is lit by the moon, and it casts a gray sheen across the roads and trees. Shadows lean over the boxed-up shapes of the homes. The swamp has really started to stink now. I'm not sure from what. Maybe the cicadas or maybe the whole place is just rotten. It's funny, though, the critters are still there. The bullfrogs howl and the crickets scream into the night sky. A cacophony of sound pools around the car, then ebbs as I drive away.

I circle through the neighborhood, then head over to Natasha's apartment building. I glance up at her window on the fourth floor. It's nearing 2:00 a.m., but the light is on. I stare at it for a little while before driving away.

Near 7:00 a.m., Brenda shows up and takes over for me. I shower in the back bathroom with the water on cold to wake me up. Sleep presses at my temples. The night has bled away into a pirate's morning with the sun sitting squat on the horizon, scarlet and spreading a blush across the sky. Usually skies like that mean a storm is coming, but there's been nothing on the weather channel to indicate it.

Three days until the anniversary.

I lather my hair with shitty shampoo, rinse, then start cleaning my feet. The deputy boots are the only thing I hate about this job, besides having to talk with the council. They're heavy and don't allow your feet to breathe. I'd rather wear tennis shoes but the one day I tried it, Mason took a look at my feet and told me if I wore them again, he'd cut them off me.

He's at his desk when I get out of the shower, my hair loose and wet around my shoulders. I don't want to get the uniform damp, but my hair is so thick that if I put it up, it'll never dry.

Then the moisture will gather with the humidity and eventually it'll start to smell like I never even took a shower.

"Boring night," I say.

"That's a good thing. Be thankful for it."

I stand in the doorframe. He sits at his desk, a topographical map of the town laid out in front of him in blue and white etchings. I move forward and the scent of the soap balloons around me. It was his. Now I smell like an old man. "What's this?"

He outlines the section of town closest to the forest, where all the farms are. "Here's where they're spraying," he says, and makes a circle with his finger. "This entire area."

"The whole thing?"

"Yep."

I look down at the map. It's a sizable area to spray. Much beyond where I think the cicadas even are. The area includes several farms who haven't been affected by the bugs. "What about Jim Kavanaugh's place? He hasn't reported anything."

"He's close enough that they included him."

I hesitate. "I have a bad feeling about this."

Mason leans back in his desk chair and it creaks under his weight. Then he reaches up and rubs his mustache. "Bad feelings don't get us anywhere," he says. "Give me a legitimate reason to stop them."

The map stares up at me, a maze of lines and inclines—the steep ledge of the forest, the elevating layers that lead to the mountains in the distance, the plateau at the edge of town, and the gully of the swamp. There is so much town and so few of us law enforcement. "They're coming at nine," I say. "At this point, there's nothing we can do to get them to stop."

He crooks his neck. "You wanna give up?"

I shrug. "Why waste time? We know how this works. Let's just focus on how we'll respond if and when something goes wrong."

Mason is quiet for a moment, and then he stands. He towers over me, his blond-brown hair rustling as he moves. He points his finger at me. He looks mad. Not irritated, but angry. He has never looked at me like this, except that one time after the strip club, when he threw me in the jail cell. It's a look of shock and disappointment. "You're too young for this crap," he says. "You have your whole life ahead of you. I don't want to see you acting like this until you're at least fifty."

His words hang in the room. After a while, I hesitate under his gaze. Force a laugh and smile. "Yeah, yeah," I say.

I gather the map with him, rolling the delicate paper up at the ends, the smell of dust and ancient things rising in the air. I pretend to listen to what he said. I act like it doesn't bother me. But he just doesn't get it and he never will. He doesn't know what it's like to look into your future and see nothing. For me, it's just the heat of the summer and the pulse of the cicadas, that steady thrumming and void that never goes away.

We drive separately out to the forest for the unveiling of the stunning agent. Mason is still mad by the time we get out and start showing everyone where the masses are located. The Feds have six cars here, along with a mega van from which suited agents with gas masks exit. They look surreal against the backdrop, these people with white, plastic looking body suits against the West Virginia sun, the surviving wheat crops gold behind them and the green of the grass brushing their feet.

Sabina wears normal clothes, which makes me feel better. She stomps around in heeled boots, giving orders. Normally, I'd find it a huge turn on. But there's something in the wind today, something low and dank that makes me feel like this is all wrong.

Tommy and Junior are here. They rode in with Mason and it was hard not to feel like an outsider, but I know Mason. He keeps the dummies close because he's a good person. Because he worries about them, about all of us.

The three of them stand in ankle-deep tobacco plant rot, staring out at the edge of the forest. We're at James's house, still empty, about a hundred feet out from the forest. The white suits stomp across the rotted plants, their bodies like splattered paint against the backdrop of the forest. I sit down on the front steps of James's porch. The wood planks beneath are warm from the sunlight. For a second, I almost doze off, but then Tommy nudges my foot with his.

"What you think is gonna happen?" he asks.

I stare up at him. He's tall, like Mason, and built like a football player. He can't run very fast but he's like a bear when perps come bursting out of a house, high on meth or whatever else. He's bionic man. Nothing gets through him. And while I can be fast when I want, I'm not invincible like he is. Perps have taken me down before, numerous times. "Don't worry," I tell him. "I'll protect you."

He makes a face. "You seen anything like this out in the city?"

I rub my face. I'm starting to get a sleep headache, and right now all I really want to think about is getting home and getting in bed. "No. They wouldn't do a big thing like this in a populated area."

"Yeah." He picks at his teeth. "Are you worried?"

Beyond him, the darkness of the trees engulfs the small white figures. A breeze carries through, lifting the leaves that have survived the decomposition that's affected the others. "I'm concerned," I admit. "But not worried."

He nods again and turns back to the scene. We've been told to stay back, but otherwise were given no instruction on what to do. It's pretty stupid to have all four of us here. If something went wrong, then the town would be left with no police force. I stand and head back to the car to wait.

"Can one of you help us out, here?" a guy in a suit asks.

I squint. He's speaking vaguely in my direction, but Tommy is there, too. I pretend I didn't hear him and sit down in the driver's seat of the car. Tommy nods in the man's direction. "What can I do you for?"

"We're trying to determine the property line."

"I can help you with that," Tommy says. He moves forward, stomping over the rot, his ass sticking out like he's someone important, makes his way toward the tree line. The people in suits are spraying now, and the hum of a motor fills the air. I half expect the cicadas to swarm us, angry and drunk on the fumes, but they don't. The sprayers spray and when I bring the binoculars to my eyes, I can see the bugs falling out of the trees in a quiet slumber. It's eerie to watch them fall like that, all quiet except for the whining sound of the machine powering the sprayers.

I turn. Mason watches with his hand shading his eyes. Tommy edges the property line, growing smaller and smaller the further he goes. He points, and then the echo of his laugh carries to us.

They spray.

I sit and watch, the sun warming my face. As strong as it is, I know the water from the storm will evaporate quickly. The streets will clear of puddles. Maybe everything's going to be okay. Maybe this will work, and the bugs won't be crazy again next year. We'll regrow everything better next summer, and the crops will return stronger than they were before.

It's strange to think like this, to look and see the positive. It seems like every time I looked forward to something positive—a life with Lena, a job I loved, spending time with my family—it's always been snatched away. But maybe things are different now.

Someone shouts.

I jump to my feet, squinting into the forest. Mason moves forward, and I follow him with my hand on my gun. The humming from the generator turns drills an eerie echo across the dead crops, tunneling across the farm.

It's just Tommy fooling around. He throws one of the dead crops into the air and laughs.

🐜

Junior and Mason head back to the precinct but Tommy and I wait until everyone is done spraying and the last batch of cicadas is tucked into the white biohazard van. "That was gay," he says. "What now?"

"Don't use gay like that." I climb into the front seat of the car. "Mason wanted us to visit the farms around here. Tell them what happened."

"Are you sure I need to be here for that?"

"I don't need you for shit, Tommy. These are Mason's orders."

The SUV rumbles to life and I peel out, leaving a trail of dust behind me. It clouds the white van, then the trees, shimmering in the early morning sunlight. Tommy gives a loud, "Yee-haw," as we turn onto the main road.

In the rearview mirror, the white van slowly recedes until the suited guys look like little dots in the distance. I pick up speed, allow myself to laugh. Everything is fine. The bugs are gone now.

Yet, for some reason, I still have this tightness in my stomach.

🐜

The first two farms are easy—families of farmers that Tommy knows well. At the second house, they bring us lemonade and invite us to sit on the porch. It's nice out there in the shade with a breeze coming in off the mountains. Their basset hound comes outside and starts to lick at my ankles. His belly drags at the floors.

We're saying goodbye when I spot a cicada resting on the porch railing. I slap at it, but it teeters off, crawling away into the half-dead cornfield next to us. "Did you fucking see that?" I ask.

"Yeah," Tommy says. "What the fuck?"

I grab my cellphone, heading back to the truck. The family is inside now and I don't want to scare them. I sit behind the wheel of the truck as Sabina's line rings and rings. It goes through to voicemail. I try again as Tommy clambers inside the truck with me. Sunlight glints across the glass. I'm starting the truck up when she finally answers.

"I just saw another cicada," I say. "I thought you were going to get rid of them."

"Jess?"

"It was sitting on someone's porch."

There's a pause on the other end of the line. I back up, then turn onto the main road, driving slowly, headed for Jim's house. "They'll pop up here and there," Sabina says. "We couldn't account for all of them, you know."

The truck hums beneath me, almost like the hum of the cicadas when they swarmed, that lulled, warm sound. "I can't tell people they're safe. We failed them."

"Nobody failed anything. That's just the way things are, Jess."

The road hums. I hold the phone to my ear a little longer, then hang up. For some reason, it bothers me. It bothers me that we've done everything we were supposed to and things still aren't quite right.

"What did she say?" Tommy asks.

"Nothing helpful."

He's silent for a moment, then, "You'll handle the next house?"

I speed down the road. The sun is at its highest now, burning through the windshield onto us. I have the air conditioning on high but it's not enough. "Why me?" I ask. My mouth is tight, and for some reason I feel like crying. "I thought you were Mr. Sunshine."

"Fuck no," he says. "Jim's weird."

"Jim's fine. You just don't know him."

We turn onto a dirt road, and head back into the forest. Jim's cabin is covered by shade. A rusting tractor rests out front where weeds grow tangled near the tires. I step outside and the sound of the marshland swallows me—crickets, frogs, the wave of the heat under the sun.

I cross through some bugleweed. The purple stalks grow up to my knees, their tangled green stalks thick and strong. They're the only things that have survived. Figures. I kick as they tangle around my boots.

"Jim?" I knock after reaching the door. Tommy stands about ten feet back. The car is behind him, shaded by the trees.

"Maybe he's not home?"

"He works night shift." I knock harder. "Jim? It's Jessica. Just want to let you know about the bug situation."

I listen but there's no answer. No sound at all from inside. My nose wrinkles. I turn to Tommy. He shrugs. "We tried."

"Call Mason and tell him I'm heading inside."

"Why?"

"I have a bad feeling."

"You can't break into someone's house based on a feeling."

Heat licks at my neck. A buzzing sound begins in my ears, heavy and warm. Peering in through the front window, I point out a joint left on the windowsill. It's been burned down to a stub, barely half an inch with the paper licked black. "Probable cause," I say. "Call Mason."

I jiggle the doorknob on the front door, but it's not even locked. Slowly, I push the door open. It's dark inside, and the smell of chemicals inundates. Then I breathe in and taste the smell. It's chemical, like how Mason smelled after leaving the hospital.

"Jim?"

No answer. I step inside and flick on the light switch. The cabin is clean, more so than I would've expected, though sparse. The wooden kitchen cabinets are peeling but the stove is clean as can be. A picture of Jim and his ex-wife rests on the only table in the room. Otherwise, there are no pictures.

I make my way into the living room, and then to the closed bedroom door. He's probably just sleeping. That's what night shift people do. They sleep in the day. But when I open the bedroom door, he's not in bed. The curtains are drawn, so it's hard to see at first. Light edges in around the corners. I pass by the bed and open the door to the bathroom.

Jim lies on the floor. His skin is pale, and his mouth is partially open. Eyes closed.

"Tommy!" I shout. "Get in here!"

I kneel down, my hand reaching for his neck to find a pulse. At first, I feel nothing. But pressing harder, I find one—though faint. I tilt his neck up and listen for sounds of breathing. There's barely any.

Tommy rushes in. "Fuck," he says. "Alive?"

"Barely."

"What do you think it was? Drugs?"

"They would've been on the floor somewhere. There's nothing. Look."

I tilt Jim's head back, trying to feel his neck for anything that might be blocking the airway.

"We can't wait for an ambulance."

"Grab his torso," Tommy says. "Under the arms."

I move around so I'm grabbing Jim by his arms, and then Tommy tells me to lift. Jim is surprisingly light. For such a solid man, it bothers me to feel him like this. He's all bone and veins, thin skin, and blood.

"Backseat," Tommy calls to me.

It's hard to maneuver him through the cabin, small as it is. I almost drop him twice, but finally we get to the car. Tommy manages to drag the back door open, so we can get him inside. "You drive," I say. "I think he stopped breathing."

I climb into the backseat while Tommy takes the driver's seat. I've barely shut the door behind me when the engine starts and then we jostle over the dead plants, swinging ass end into the road before straightening out.

I shift so I'm kneeling on the SUV floor, hovering over Jim's lanky body. His eyes are closed, and when I feel him second time, there's no breath coming from his nose. His pulse is light and shallow. I lean down, pinch his nose and open his mouth.

Breathing for another person takes a lot of energy. I've only had to do it once before, and it was hard to keep going. The man was bigger than me, like Jim is, with large lungs to fill. I breathe in as deeply as possible, exhale into his mouth. Then administer chest compressions. I do the routine again—inhale, exhale the breath into his still body.

Tommy gains speed quickly, and I can hear the road change as we find pavement. "Keep going," he says. "Keep him breathing."

I try. Inhale, exhale, press. Jim's not breathing for himself at all and his heartbeat is almost not there. It's like I'm not pressing hard enough. Something is wrong. I press harder on the chest compressions. His skin is not how it should be. It's cold when it should be warm, and for the first time I wonder how long he's been like this. Maybe an hour? Maybe more. Maybe since we sprayed that damn chemical across the trees.

I crouch. Breathe in, exhale into his mouth. My own breath has weakened from breathing for him. Every time I suck in more air, I feel more and more tired, but I keep going because it's Jim. Because I know him, and he knew my sister. Because I don't want him to give up yet.

It's a fifteen-minute ride into town but it feels like hours.

We get to the hospital and a gurney immediately rolls up to greet us. Hospital warning lights flash. Then, the side door to the SUV opens and one of the doctors pulls Jim onto a gurney. His eyes stay shut. His body is like rubber being placed into position, and then someone yells at me to move, so I do, stepping out onto the concrete of the hospital parking lot. My knees my give out. I sit down on the concrete.

They wheel Jim inside the hospital, and Tommy follows him. I'm exhausted. My heart beats sluggishly. A nurse settles next to me with her hands on my shoulders and asks me if I'm okay, but it's like I'm hearing her through a tunnel. Then it's just the sound of the whining machine back at the farm, that high-pitched buzzing, and I bring my hands to my ears and cover them.

ELEVEN

IT'S LATE WHEN MASON DRIVES ME HOME. After he leaves, I
sit outside on the porch with a bottle of whiskey I picked up at
the shopping center. I walked over after the doctors came outside to tell me Jim was dead.

The sun fades. I sip the whiskey directly from the bottle, laz-
ing around in the broken sun chair my mom had for years. One
of the arms slopes downward too steeply and one of the rungs
near the foot of the chair has snapped, leaving a belt-sized hole
in it.

They called Jim's death at 3:25 p.m. Meg died at 10:31. Mom
and Dad were dead on impact, probably sometime around 8:00
a.m. They were headed for breakfast and then were going to
meet me halfway between here and DC for the afternoon. Meg
had a new boyfriend, a guy she was serious with who lived a few
towns over. He offered to drive her out that day, but she said no,
she wanted to spend time with the family.

The sun starts to warm me, so I strip out of my uniform and
sit there in my bra and underwear, sipping smooth Johnnie
Walker. The sun is searing, even at the end of the day like this,
and for some reason, the pain pleases me. I look out into the
woods, scanning the tree line like it all means something, but it
doesn't mean anything.

I think about Natasha and my fingers itch for my phone. I
grab it, open a browser. I'm drunk. I know because the outside

feels hazy, my blood hot under my skin. A pulse of shame beats through me. I force it away.

My favorite porn site is bookmarked, and I pull it up, scrolling through. There's nobody that reminds me of Natasha. They don't have porn girls with goofy smiles and freckled skin, with curly, springy hair, and too-serious eyes, and a large laugh. It surprises me how much I'm okay with that. How, in this moment, I want nothing to do with her.

I click into a video. My body is already tensed, heated. I shove the feeling down, sipping more whiskey. It's sweet now, like licorice. The leaves sway in the breeze as my heart beats, light and erratic.

※

I retire to Meg's room to sleep, and Natasha comes to me in the not-quite-real moments before waking. I'm lying on my side on the bed, the covers bunched at my feet. Sunlight warms the floorboards through the window. The light hangs there, golden and alight with dust, suspended in the beam. The ceiling crouches low in the corner with the natural slope of the roof, coming to rest just a foot above my head.

Natasha rests on her side, facing me. She's on top of the covers, not under them, and the bloom of natural light behind her makes her skin look tan and sparkling. Her eyes are open. I reach out and tuck a curl behind her ear.

"The tree's rotting," she says. "It's too bad."

"Which tree?"

"The oak in the front of the house."

I stare at her. She looks like she's been awake for a long time. Young and sprightly in a way I haven't felt in ages. "It's not rotting," I say. "I just checked it."

The world feels coated in golden light. It's in the wood walls of the cabin, the sunshine that pours in around us. The bed shifts, and then Natasha's hand is on my waist, and her lips are on my neck. She's feather-light and smells like lavender. I close my eyes, but when I wake up, there's nobody there.

The precinct doesn't feel like the precinct in the morning. I get there around 9:00 a.m., and the parking lot is packed with cars. Reporters line the sidewalk leading inside. All the noise and commotion spring a feeling of tight panic in my chest. It's not like it used to be. I used to love big crowds. That's why I loved DC. I could disappear in them. No one knew me, and no one knew my past.

Brushing past the crowd, I tuck my chin, not making eye contact with anyone, and push my way inside. The smell of freshly cut flowers blooms around me as soon as I walk into the main room. I glance up. A bouquet of lilies and sunflowers rest on the countertop near the comm desk. Brenda is there. Mason stands in the corner on the landline, talking loudly.

Two days left until the anniversary.

I make my way over to Brenda. Someone has made a pot of fresh coffee and brought some apple cinnamon donuts. I don't feel much like eating, but I pour myself a cup of coffee and stand next to her. "Want me to pour you some?"

"I've had enough." Her eyes crease in the corner, heavy with fatigue. "You okay?"

I force a smile. "Where's Tommy?"

"Took the day. I think that was his first dead one."

"The first is always the hardest," I say.

Brenda's opening her mouth as Mason slams down the landline and lets out a string of curses. He turns. His hair is disheveled, his eyes red. I can feel the tension in him just by looking at him. "You're here," he says.

"What can I do?"

He exhales, then wipes at his mustache with his palm. "Feds are coming to the station in a few hours. I need you over at the coroner's. See if you can get an official cause of death."

I holster my gun and badge at my side. "I doubt they'll have anything."

"Just try."

A weight drops over me. I don't want to see Jim's lifeless body today. I don't want to go to the morgue. I want to go back to yesterday when there was still a chance for him to work out his problems, and maybe call up his ex-wife, and have a shot. It's just unfair. His life was short and hard, and now he's dead.

"And Jess?"

"What?"

"Get Natasha over here. I can't deal with those fuckers outside."

Pain pricks at my chest. I pick up Jim's case file from the desk. It's thin. Only a few sheets of paper. I wonder if Mason wrote it up, or if Brenda did. I bet my life it was her. She's strong like that. She lost a child years ago, a boy. She still carries that look about her, though. It's something that, once you've been through it, you can't get rid of.

Sometimes I look at pictures of myself before the crash, before Lena left, and it seems like my face is different. It's tighter, more pert. I was prettier back then. Now, I look at pictures of myself and I look like someone heavy. My features tilt down now. My eyes don't sparkle anymore. "I'll take care of it," I say.

I gather my things and head out the back door where the sheriff's SUV is parked. It usually gives me immense pleasure to drive around in it but today, everything feels hollow. I pass the park, still empty looking from the storm. The entire town looks empty now, all broken and quiet.

I go to the coroner's first, in the basement of the hospital. It smells like formaldehyde in there, like my seventh-grade science classroom. The stench almost gags me as I walk in. I take a few shallow breaths, coughing like that will expel some of the particles, but it lingers there in my throat. "How do you live like this?" I ask.

The coroner shrugs. "You get used to it. I don't even smell it anymore."

"I'd hate to come home to you at the end of the day."

"The feeling is mutual." He picks up a clipboard and walks over to a wall of metal, opening a square door to pull out a gurney with a white sheet over it. Metal clicks. He pulls back the sheet to reveal Jim's corpse. His skin is gray now, so different from the reds and pinks that trembled across his body yesterday. A line cuts down the center of his chest, where he was cut open for autopsy. "From what I can tell, he had a reaction to something."

"To what?"

"I'm running tests on the substances found in his lungs, but they might not be back for a while."

"The Feds are coming today," I say. "I need to know if it had something to do with the chemical agent they released. There were no drugs except marijuana at the house."

"He tested negative for all the major stuff—cocaine, heroin."

"So, it was the chemicals?"

"I didn't say that."

I stare at him. The lights are low down here, making his skin look more yellow than white, and for some stupid reason it reminds me of Natasha. "Accidental, but still. Their agent killed him."

"I'll know for sure by tomorrow."

He busies himself with his papers and frustration builds in my chest. All I want is to know what happened so I can keep it from happening again. If I don't know, then I can't do anything about it. If I had known it was storming that day Meg was coming to visit, I would've called it off. That's part of being a cop—mitigating risk. I used to think I did it well.

"I just need to know why," I say.

"I'll give you a call tomorrow, Jessica."

I look down at Jim. He seems so fake, like a wax doll. It's hard to believe he ever occupied that body. It's just an empty shell, and for a second, I wonder if his soul is still lingering around town, like I feel Meg's is sometimes, watching his ex-wife curl her hair in the mirror, or sitting at an empty barstool downtown. Maybe he's back at the house where I found him, resting outside on the porch, just listening to the bugs hiss and taking some sweet sunshine.

It takes me three tries to go to Natasha's office. At first, the new security guard doesn't let me in. Then, for a few minutes, I think maybe it's a sign and I shouldn't see her. But just as I'm about to walk away, Mason's voice and the red lines in his eyes come back to me.

By the time I walk down the hall to her office, I'm shaking. I knock on the door, half expecting her to be in a meeting somewhere, but she answers with a short, "Come in."

I open the door to dim light.

Natasha always works in the dark. She'll pull the curtains back during the day, letting the sunshine pour in, and then after it sets, she'll forget to turn on the lights inside the room. She sits in shadows. I flip the light switch on and she turns to look at me.

Her mouth immediately tightens. "Jess."

"Mason wants you at the station."

She sits at her desk, legs stretched out, one slung over the other. She wears pants today, sky blue things that pull tight around her waist, and a black blouse. "I heard what happened with Jim. Are you okay?"

"I'm fine. Mason wants you to deal with the press."

"I heard you resuscitated him."

"He died at the hospital."

Her hair looks shorter and I don't like it. I don't like anything about her appearance right now. "Jess, I can't imagine."

A well of emotion sweeps over me, drenching my chest. I clear my throat but it's already so tight, it's hard to talk. "Are you coming, or not? Mason needs you."

She looks at me that same way she looked at me fifteen years ago in Meg's room, and it infuriates me. I turn away, placing my hand on the doorway. I hear her rise, and then a shuffling sound as she grabs for her purse. "I can't stay for long." Her keys jingle.

"I'll drive," I tell her.

"You're sure?"

"You won't be able to get through the crowd."

Natasha puts her hand on my shoulder. The heat of her palm is warm through my uniform. For a second, I imagine I'm her girlfriend and I'm picking her up for a lunch date out. I'm taking her to the Thai place out on the edge of town that she likes so much. Everything is good, and no one has just died. Picking up a pretty girl is a normal part of my day, every day.

She removes her hand. "I'm happy to help any time," she says, but her voice is stiff, like it's something she has to say, and she doesn't really mean it.

We head out, her heels clacking against the tile. There's no one else in the hallway, unlike usual. The whole hall has a hushed, quiet feel today. Usually, it's packed. Kids, legislators, council members.

"You're still mad at me?" she asks.

I crane my neck to look at her. "I wasn't mad. I was disappointed."

She's quiet. Her heels click. I can feel this wanting in her. Natasha needs for things to be good, to be happy. She needs people to like her. I've seen her before, sucking up to someone she doesn't even care about, just because she wants to be liked.

We round the corner and enter the front hall. Sunshine gleams through the open windows. Beyond it, the trees stoop, browned, broken from the storm, the run-off still muddying the streets. It doesn't look like the same town. When we step outside, my ears strain to hear the hum of the cicadas, but there is nothing, not even the chirp of crickets from the swamp.

Natasha is not the best public speaker. She's too soft, especially during press conferences, which is strange, considering she'll practically fight anyone who disagrees with her in person. When she faces the council, she's like Caesar Brutus, hacking her way through dissenters. Today, it's hard to believe she's that same person.

Her microphone is on high as she delivers the address outside, competing with the wind and the creak of the few trees that are still alive. Mason stands at her side. She looks tiny in comparison to him. A few months ago, I would've looked at the two of them and seen an angel and a devil. But now I see them and realize there is some self-centeredness in Natasha that I didn't pick up on at first. And in Mason, a sweetness.

"The preliminary autopsy report states that Jim died from a chemical reaction to an unknown toxin. Further results will be available tomorrow to see if the toxin was the same substance released into the forest yesterday morning."

I glance around. Most of the reporters are quiet, no doubt straining to hear her. A few chatter among themselves. Mark is there in a navy suit and tie. He nods at me. I glare back until he looks away.

"The sheriff's department doesn't believe the public is at risk, and that Jim's reaction was due to a specific allergy. No one else in the vicinity of the spray was affected."

"Did the spray work?"

She nods. "The cicadas were stunned, bagged, and removed."

"What about the trees?" someone asks. "Why are they dying?"

Mason turns to me for help. I step forward, brushing past Natasha to reach the microphone. "Cicadas release something called honey dew when they brood. It's harmless to humans but destroys the trees they nest in. We think the rot is so widespread this year because there were so many of them, and because they were larger than normal."

The audience is silent. I become distinctly aware of the fact that everyone is looking at me; looking at me for the first time since I was fired. I step back from the podium and move to the side.

"When did Ms. LeGrand become a deputy again?" one of Mark's reporters asks. "The last I heard, she overdosed in some club and was removed from her position."

Heat stains my cheeks. I turn away from the reporters, my heartbeat rising in my chest. Mason's voice carries through the microphone. "This office needed help and asked for her assistance. We're lucky she considered coming back." His voice is low and calm, and for a second, I flash back to high school. My dad is standing me up in front of him before the junior prom, telling me it's okay to go alone because I'm good enough. That girls in college are going to be crazy for me. That I'm pretty in a suit, that everything is going to be better once I grow up.

A chorus of questions rains down over the crowd, and then Brenda takes my arm and leads me back inside, Mason just behind us. My cheeks are still in flames. The same ringing sound punctures my ear, high and whiny like the sound of the machine that powered those sprayers yesterday.

Brenda sits at the comm desk, but I keep walking. I walk until I get to my old office and step inside, shutting the door behind me. I sit down with my back against the side of my old desk and I start to cry. I'm useless. It was my fault Jim didn't survive, that someone else would've been enough to save him, but I'm not. I'm someone who hurts people, and that's why everyone hates me so much.

I cover my face with my hands and focus on breathing in and out, in and out, like my dad taught me. Calm, calm. I try to focus on the words, but my heart is still racing, and I keep picturing that reporter's smug face as he asked the question.

I'm breathing hard when the door to the office opens. I inhale, trying to slow my tears. I figure it's Mason, but then I smell the perfume, and hear the soft inhale of her breath. I know it's Natasha without even looking. I would know her presence anywhere.

She sits down next to me and the heat of her body presses against mine. Her arm goes around my shoulders and the smell of her powder deodorant washes over me. My body tenses. She pulls me close. "Don't let them do this to you, Jess."

I swallow and wipe my face. My tears burn, tinted with mascara. "I'm never going to fit in here."

"You're amazing," she says. "You've always been a rockstar."

I laugh. "Then why don't you want me?"

A beat passes. I busy myself with wiping my face. It was the wrong thing to say but I don't care. "I think you're awesome," she says carefully. "You know that."

"And?"

She sighs. Removes her arm. We sit like that: me tilted to look at her, and her with her back resting against the side of the desk.

It's cold in the room. Vents stir the air above us. The sweat on the back of my neck has dried and now it pulls, prickly and taut, along my skin.

Finally, I lean back against the desk next to her. I look down at the skin along her arms. Pale and freckled. Natasha is heavy-boned. Not large, but there's something about her structure that makes her appear taller than she actually is. I scan her arms, her legs. They lay outstretched. I realize then how lopsided our friendship is. She doesn't spend a single extra second thinking about me, wondering what my day was like, or how I'm feeling. I rotate in and out for her. She forgets me when I'm not around. She will never care for me the way I care for her. "Sorry," I say. My whole body aches. "You don't need to explain yourself."

She cranes her neck to look at me. A sparkle takes over her eyes. "I miss you at work."

"I bet."

"I'm serious. I liked it better when you were there."

"Because I'm so pretty."

She lets out a laugh. "This is true."

We sit. The air conditioning hums off, and with the noise of it gone, I can hear the hustle in the hallway, Mason's voice rising above the static of the comms. I want to be angry like he is, but I can't. I realize then that I cannot spend a single second more crying and begging and howling for Natasha's love. I can't sit around here waiting for things to change, like being here will bring Mom and Dad and Meg back. "I know you have to get back to work," I say.

She turns to look at me. I hold her gaze for a moment, and then she smiles. It's the first time she smiles at me and I don't feel like smiling back.

TWELVE

THE FEDS SHOW UP ABOUT AN HOUR LATER. It's Sabina, two lawyers, and someone I think is in PR, even though he never specifically states what his position is. They also have some kind of investigator with them. All five of them wear suits and carry briefcases, except Sabina who struts in canvas pants and heeled wedges with what looks like a large shoulder purse. They sit at the precinct conference table, the one we never use. No one's ever been here for a conference, at least not since I started working here. We never had a big case like this before. Before, it was all drug overdoses and domestic violence complaints. Theft. Simple assault. Everything is different now, and nothing can go back to how it was.

"We can't do much until the tox screen comes back," Sabina says. "It could've been anything."

"Like what?" Mason asks.

"Drugs. An allergy to pollen."

"Right after your chemical was released?" I ask. I shift in the chair and it creaks, the wheels screaming briefly before falling silent again. "I doubt that."

Sabina meets my eye and I hold it. She wears lipstick today—blood red. It looks good with her coloring. She knows how to match and always looks put-together. Before the crash, I would've found it attractive. Now, I just look at her and think of all the ways she could break my heart. "I can't even express how sorry I am this happened," she says. "And if it was something to do with us, we'll do everything we can to make it right."

My chest constricts. I stand up from my seat and walk to the windows of the precinct. The press has fled, and the parking lot is empty. Run-off still lingers in the gutters, small streams. We'll have to dig up the old beech tree on the edge of the property. It's brown, muddied by the rain and the cicadas. I wonder if, in a few days, my oak tree at home will limp and brown, then wither and dry up.

"If it was related, it was most likely a specific internal reaction," Sabina continues. "We couldn't have predicted it."

I stand there at the window, arms crossed. Then Brenda speaks. "What are you going to do to make sure it doesn't happen again?"

"It won't," Sabina says.

"And the dead trees? What do you suggest we do about them?"

"You'll want to dig them up and plant new ones. They're no good to the forest anymore."

The phone rings. I turn. Brenda is already rising but I wave for her to sit and answer it myself. I pick it up on the fourth ring, pressing the cool plastic to my cheek. "Sheriff's office."

Someone clears their voice on the other end. "Jessica?"

"Yeah."

"It's Mark."

My stomach falls. "You want Mason?"

"No. Actually, I was hoping to talk to you."

I stiffen. "Why?"

He's quiet for a moment. Then, "Saw you were back on the force. I was thinking about doing an article on you. You've been through a lot."

The words hang there. My first reaction is to tell him to fuck off and hang up the phone. There's really no benefit for him to talk to me. He must've felt pressured—by Natasha, no doubt—

to either smooth things over with me or do something to make me feel better. "I appreciate that," I say, "but I'm not interested in talking to you."

"What if someone else did the interview?"

I exhale. Prickles of sweat threaten along my neck. "I don't need your newspaper spinning tales about my life."

"We're just going to tell your story."

"You don't care about my story, Mark. You just want to make a stir in town. You don't care about actually changing things, nor do you care about me as a person or anything I've gone through."

Mark is silent and for a second, I wonder if I've made a mistake. If he really is a nice guy who cares. But then I think about him fucking Natasha, him eating dinner at Natasha's kitchen table, him waking up to her, him sitting on the couch with her, and the feeling ebbs. "I'm sorry you feel like that," he finally says. "But I thought I'd try."

"Why don't you run a story on the man that just died? He wasn't a bad person, and he didn't deserve this. I'd like to see you guys do him some justice, if you're able."

I hang up. My hand lingers on the phone, and then I turn back toward the conference table.

🐜

The investigator asks to see the scene where everything happened, so I drive him out to Jim's house with Sabina and Mason. The three of them tromp through the dead leaves, past the bugleweed, until they're inside the tiny cabin. Their voices pool in the small space, spilling through an open window.

I wander beyond the house, deeper into the forest. All his stuff is still here, and I can't help thinking about what will happen to it. Jim had no one on the extended family list; no one to call in case of death. He didn't even have an emergency contact listed on the release form he filled out at the warehouse.

My boots kick up dirt as I make my way into the tree line, carrying the rifle in my right hand, even though there's no real reason to have it. The air is cooler under here, shaded by the leaves and branches. Light tunnels in through breaks in the overhang, like spotlights beaming down onto the forest floor. It smells like pine and something faintly chemical. The dirt on the ground has been trudged up from the Feds.

If I kept walking, the forest would slowly round up, higher and higher in elevation until reaching Spruce Knob at almost five thousand feet. The air would thin, grow colder. Up there, spruce and ash trees bloom, along with blueberry thickets. Bogs hide between ranges of rhododendron and laurel.

I'm reaching out to touch the tree when a sound in the forest stops me. It sounds like a rustle, like a bug burrowing under a paper-thin leaf. I search the forest floor. It goes quiet, then surfaces again. I spot a moving leaf a few feet to my left and make my way over, walking as quietly as possible. From behind me, Mason's voice booms through the open window. Arguing. I keep moving forward. Hot air and shadows pool around me, stifling in the stillness of the woods.

As I approach, the leaf stops moving. With the end of the rifle I flip the leaf over. Underneath it lies a single cicada. It's blue tinted, almost cerulean in the darkness of the trees. Its eyes are red. The antennae twitch at me, and for a second, I remember being a kid, looking at these things and being fascinated. I remember reading about them in the school library and presenting a report on them in science class. They were so cool, I thought. Like aliens nesting on a new planet.

I bring the rifle up. Sight the creature. Shoot.

The bullet blows right through the bug. It splatters, a mesh of exoskeleton and bug juice, across the dirt. Mason's voice bellows through the air and not long after, footsteps crash through the overgrowth behind me. Rapid breaths. Then he's there, one hand on my shoulder, the other reaching for the rifle. "What happened?" he asks.

I give him the rifle and point to the desiccated cicada.

"Everything okay?" Sabina asks.

The forest creaks, so large and silent it could eat me alive. "You missed one," I reply.

Two days later, I put the house on the market. I don't think about it much, just click and post and there it is online, ready for anyone to take as their own. After staring at it for a little while, Mason calls me down to the precinct. We've gotten the results back on the drug found in Jim's system. It's a cannabinoid, though unidentified. Not the substance used to get rid of the bugs. "He had a bad reaction," the medical examiner says. "He probably didn't know what was in the drugs. It just happened."

He rules cause of death and I head out to Jim's place one more time. Tommy comes with me. Jim didn't have a will and the house was in his name, completely paid off. I called the ex-wife to see if she wanted to come over and take some of his things, but she didn't.

From the front porch of the cabin, I call a realtor and a junker. The junker gets there first. They park on top of the bugleweed, smashing the blue flowers into the ground with a large tire, treaded with muck and dirt the color of rust. It's cooler today, but both the men in the truck are sweating as they step out of the cab.

"What's going?" they ask.

"Everything."

The two of them look at each other for a moment, then back at me. "You're sure?"

"Yes."

The trees sway overhead. It feels wrong to throw an entire man's life out, but I'm not sure what else to do.

While the junkers are working, I wander into the garage. I've never been in here before. It smells like dust and grime. Rays of light filter through dirty windows. I move to the back where a row of old Indian motorcycles rests. There are four of them, and two are covered by burlap bags. The one closest to the wall looks the newest. It's not coated in dust like the rest. Maroon-colored, the handles stretch, recently polished.

I back it out of its spot.

It's an Indian Chief, a newer version. I only know because Lena used to ride. She taught me in an elementary school parking lot one evening but I never got my license for it. I figured she would be around to drive us whenever I wanted.

After managing to open the garage door, I pull the bike out into the dim shade of the day. The heat hangs heavy out here, tinted with moisture from the undergrowth. It's like living in a rainforest. I run my hand over the handles, the sleek body frame.

"What you got there?" Tommy asks.

"Bike."

"Looks good on you."

"I'm thinking of buying it off the estate."

He squints. He looks smaller than he did two days ago. Life has pushed him down in size, like it does after a death. Still, there's something distinctly hopeful in him. A lingering optimism. I look at him and see a young boy, someone whose entire future is ahead of him. "Do it," he says.

"Let's see if it works first."

I hop on the seat. Kick up the footrest. It takes me two tries to start it—I'm not used to manual—but then the engine kicks in, purring between my legs. The vibrations spread through my gut and chest. The sound of it is sharp and loud and alive in the heat of the forest. When I turn to look at Tommy, he's smiling.

I tell Tommy I'm not going to be working for the rest of the day. It's the anniversary, after all. I turn my phone off and tuck it in my pocket, then go speeding off on Jim's bike.

The air is hot for a ride, but not terrible for this time in the summer. I cruise into town, stopping at the stop sign by the Stone. I pass the post office, then start to rise in elevation as I head out of town. I pass my cabin, and the trees grow denser. It takes me a couple miles to figure out the gears, but by the time I'm headed out of town, I've got it. I increase my speed, taking the turns sharp like Lena taught me, feeling the sun burn down on my cheeks.

The Alleghenies rise in front of me. The second growth forest is dense and dark; fir and ash trees grow rampant over rhododendron and laurel that spring up along the river side. As the road rises in elevation, the air grows cooler. I keep going until the river narrows with boulders. Sweat sticks to my skin as I slow and pull over on the side of the road. I stash the bike amongst some bushes and climb down the encampment to the water bed.

It's pebbly down here with a surprisingly low tide considering the rain we've had. It smells like fresh water, the scent you get from tall mountain run-off. Clean and crisp. I love that smell, the chill of it. That was how it smelled when I hiked Mount Snow in undergrad. It was like the snow was in the very air itself; I could taste it.

I find a large boulder to sit on and take my shoes off, dabbling my feet in the water. I brought two vodka nips with me and take them out, look at them. They shimmer in the light. After a moment, I place them back inside my uniform pocket.

It's still hot, even at a higher elevation.

The trees sway. The foliage is dense here at the S-curve of the river. The shoulders run tight. A few feet away, the current eddies in a shallow pool of slow-moving water. I check around me, then start to strip.

Dad would never approve of this, but Mom and Meg would. The three of us used to swim everywhere. In lakes, rivers, the ocean. On one trip to Rodanthe, North Carolina, Mom forced my dad to stop on the side of the road so the three of us could get in the water. I was seven. Meg was fourteen.

"It's perfect right in this spot," my mom said. "If we drive any further, it might not be this good again."

My dad complained for a moment before stopping for her. Meg helped me take off my clothes and the three of us went frolicking in the cool water in our underwear. I remember the waves were stronger than I thought. They crashed into my gangly, skinny body, battering my skin and stinging my eyes. I dove under the waves again and again. There was something soothing about being beneath them. The whole world went quiet and dark and smooth.

That's how it feels now as I lean back into the shallow pool, letting my hair get caught in the current. I can hear the tinkle of water and fish and rock just beneath the surface. I stretch my arms out and lift my feet, floating. I look up at the trees and underbrush. For a moment, a flicker of movement catches my eye. I panic, sloshing forward in the water so I'm standing on my own two feet again.

Water drips from my hair, like a million caterpillars cascading down my body. I squint into the underbrush, trying to spot the whisper of cicada wings, anything. I search and search, walking over to the side of the river but I never find anything. It's only when a car passes by on the road that I realize I'm crying. There are no cicadas out. There are barely mosquitos.

I am alone.

I close my eyes. I wish everything would go back to the way it was. I wish I was still fifteen, sitting across the table from my sister and her best friend, this pretty girl I thought might look at me someday like I was more than what I was. I want that back so badly it hurts.

But it has been two years now and I am still stuck on this town and that house and those moments that ruined my life. If I'm going to keep going, I have to tuck them away somehow, to keep Meg with me without letting her absence be everything, to let her lingering bolster me.

I force myself to relax. I sink back down into the water, still crying, but less so now. I lean back and float again, so all I can do is hear the tinkle of the current.

I imagine Dad is complaining about the heat from the side of the road. Mom is further upstream, looking for small fish. It's quiet and peaceful. There is nothing here that can harm me. I open my eyes. In the sliver of sunlight, I can almost see Meg next to me. Her tiny nose is spotted with freckles. She wrinkles it, placing one of her hands under my neck and the other under my legs. "Stop flailing, Jessie," she says. "I got you."

She helps keep me afloat. She always has and she always will.

THIRTEEN

A MONTH PASSES. A string of serious storms rattles the area, flooding the swamp and several houses near downtown. I get an AmeriCorps crew to remove the remaining dead trees and replace them with new ones. The town looks better, but the stink of the rot lingers. It's worse near the bogs, but there's nothing we can do about it.

Mason hires me full-time, and I'm finally able to return my stupid security uniform. I stop seeing Natasha. She texts me for about two weeks after I switch positions, then falls silent. I start buying groceries in a neighboring town. After work, I go straight home and continue my projects on the house. I see the cicadas here and there and make weekly calls to Sabina, but she never tells me what I want to hear.

At the end of August, I receive an invite to attend a luncheon hosted by the mayor. The letter says they are honoring five people for "outstanding service to the Mayberry community." At first, I think it's a prank, so I call Brenda. She's working late at the station, and the static of the comms buzzes in the background as she answers her phone.

"What the fuck," I say. "How can I find out who did this?"

Brenda laughs. "It's not a prank. That's a real thing."

"Then how come I've never heard of it before?"

"Because you don't pay attention to anything that happens around this town unless it concerns you."

I sigh into the phone. It's not too late, but the sun is already burning low on the horizon, casting a golden sheen over the trees. I watch it set from the porch, seated in mom's old chair with a hand-rolled cigarette trailing smoke into the breeze. "I'm incredibly offended," I say. "So, it's real?"

"Very real. I'm glad you got it this year."

"I don't get why."

Brenda exhales. "I know you like to think everyone around here hates you, but there are some of us who don't, honey."

A small smile graces my lips. I haven't smiled in a while. Probably since the last time I talked to Natasha. We were texting. She told me she got in a yelling match with one of the other council members and ended up leaving in a haste. The mayor sought her out after to tell her what a good job she was doing and how he appreciates having her voice and input.

"Jessica?"

"Yeah," I say. "Well, thanks. I appreciate you."

I end the call, looking over the invitation. It's made from cardstock, like a wedding invitation. The words are done in curly, gold font. I turn it to the back where there's a schedule for the luncheon, including the names of the four other people being honored.

My gaze zooms in on one.

Natasha.

Fuck. It feels like my stomach has shot through the chair, and it takes a second for me to recover. Then I pick up the cigarette from the chair armrest and bring it to my lips. It tastes like wood, faint licorice. I won't go, I tell myself. There's no need. It's all just a bunch of baloney anyway. But then I think about Mason, and about Brenda. They must've done some work to nominate me.

What really decides it for me is Natasha. I picture her showing up in one of those dresses she likes to wear, the heels. When

I lie in bed at night, I always picture her. I think about the way her skin felt, and how she tasted, and the sounds she made when we were together.

I tuck the invitation under my leg and lean back.

The oak tree is still alive. I've checked the bark for signs of decay almost every day, but it stands tall and strong. Still, I worry I'll run outside in the morning to see it limping over the grasses and weeds. It fills me with dread, but at the same time, I know that nothing can survive forever.

The day of the luncheon, I dress in a black suit with a low-cut white shirt. I drape a silver necklace along my breastbone and wear heels for the first time since I lived in DC. Mason's sister is visiting, and he gets her to agree to come with me. She shows up at my house at eleven thirty in a white summer dress with flowers on it. She's younger than Mason, but not by much. In her mid-forties, the type of woman I'd normally go for. Her name is Maggie. She's a redhead. Short with a thick stomach and beautiful breasts, full lips.

We get to the luncheon and she immediately orders me a mimosa, then sits with her own, looking at me with a smile. She has beautiful, pouty lips, and the kind of smirk that reminds me of Natasha so much I could cry. "On a scale from one to ten, how uncomfortable are you right now?"

I sip the mimosa. We sit inside a fancy brunch restaurant, next to a row of large windows. It's hot, so I've taken my jacket off and sit in my sleeveless top and pants. White tableclothed tables sit around a stage and podium. Lilies hang in a long lei around hanging lights. There are at least a hundred other people here. "The scale stops at ten?" I ask.

Maggie laughs. "Mason told me you were like this."

"Like what?"

"Nervous."

"I'm really fine." I drain the rest of the mimosa in one sip and smile at her. She smiles back. And it feels good. It feels nice. But my smile is there because I put it there. Not like with Natasha where my smile would just slip out, almost like I couldn't control it.

"You want another?" She slides hers over to me. "I'll get more."

She leaves, and I stare at the glass but don't drink it. It's fancy champagne. The kind I could drink for hours and not get sick off if I wanted, but I don't. I sit back in my seat at the table they've assigned me and look around. A large cake rests in the corner. Waiters in ties ferry about the room, handing out hors d'oeuvres.

I'm itching for a second glass of champagne when a voice comes from behind me. "Well, look at you, Rockstar."

I crane my neck. Turn. Natasha stands there, Mark at her side. She's in a white dress, too, but something more formal than Maggie. It tapers around her stomach, the fabric thick and smooth along her skin. Her hair curls tightly. She wears eyeliner. She never wears eyeliner. And then I spot the emerald- and diamond-encrusted rock on her ring finger.

My heart drops. A rush of feeling floods through me, so strong I almost think I'm going to pass out. I put my hand on the table. Pain wracks my body. I force myself to smile. "Hey, there."

"I'm so glad you're here," Natasha says. "I thought you might not show up."

Shaking, I rise. It feels like someone has just shot me in the gut. "Mason made me." I hold out my hand. "How are you, Mark?"

There's a second where he pauses, staring at me, and I stare back, my hand extended. Then he reaches out and clasps my hand. I squeeze back as hard as I can. It feels like my eyes are watering when I pull away. "Things are good," he says. "How are they with you?"

I nod to Natasha's ring. "Not as good as they are with you, apparently."

Mark laughs. "Happened a week ago. I'm a lucky guy."

Heat branches across my chest, no match for the air conditioning ruffling the lip of my blouse. I'm about to congratulate them when Maggie shows up with two more mimosas in her hand. She gives me one, then turns to Mark and Natasha. "Hi." She holds out her hand. "I'm Maggie."

She and Mark start talking about copy editing and working for local presses. I hold the drink to my chest. My eyes stay on Natasha. After a while, she turns and locks eyes with me. Her lips spread into a line and her eyes are glossy, probably from a mimosa or two. I wonder if her love for Mark is real or if she's doing this because that's what she thinks she's supposed to do. Because she's Natasha and she has this stubborn, committed outlook on what her life is going to be like, a picture in her head of the way things are destined to happen.

I turn away from her just as the first speaker steps up to the microphone and asks everyone to find their seats. Maggie sits down, and I take my place next to her. Natasha sits with Mark at the table in front of us so I'm staring at the back of her head and her arms, free of fabric. I haven't seen her arms exposed in public like this since she was in college. I remember back then, she was a bit pudgier. More childlike. Now, she's full on woman. This astute, snarky thing that no one dares to argue with. I stare at her curls, her back.

She shifts, and then for a moment it feels like the whole world slows down. She turns around. Everyone else is still, staring face forward at the speaker. Natasha and I lock gazes. A moment passes. I want to tell her it's okay. That she can let go. I am not the same girl who cried every night over Lena. I'm not the girl who couldn't face a morning without a glass of whiskey.

Natasha holds my gaze for another moment. Then she tucks a curl of her hair behind her ear and turns away.

After dropping Maggie at Mason's house, I drive the old route home. Rocks kick up under my car. It smells like pine, like normal. I kick the corners, speeding up when I should slow down. It reminds me of high school, curving back home after prom, all cried out of tears after sitting there all night long, wanting to dance with someone but finding no one.

I get home and park the car. The crickets sing their song, high and sweet. It smells like grass and summer, the heat of the sun that lingers in baked earth. I love this house, these woods. But even with the job, even with the award, with Mason, Brenda, this place is haunted.

The only thing that makes it better is the ranger supervisor training I'm going to next week in DC. Sabina called me a few weeks ago and told me about the job it's for. I'll be working out west in the state parks as a ranger. They haven't decided where to place me yet, but most likely it'll be in Yellowstone National Park.

I've cleaned the house up, trying to get something to feel right so I can leave it without worrying. I finished the insulation. I cleaned up the outside, shearing down the trees. The yard sits plucked free of weeds, green in a bloom of rain that's fallen across the area. Haze lingers over the grass, a warm ray of moisture from the wetness of the earth.

After dropping my things off in the bedroom, I head downstairs. I take out some whiskey and pour it in a shot glass. Set it on the counter and stare at it but don't drink it. More and more lately, I keep pouring myself drinks I don't drink. I've been running every day, training my body back to how it used to be. I still wake up with this pain in my chest, though. It strikes me out of the blue sometimes.

A warm breeze fetters in through the kitchen window, tinted with my mom's perfume. I head for my parents' room. Everything is still here, exactly where I left it, like it's always been.

I walk through the bedroom to the porch and open the door. Hot air blasts me in the face. It smells like grass and wet dirt, like the days after the crash, and everything that hurts bad.

I lie down flat, so my back is pressed into the wood planks, and close my eyes. The heat won't leave until October. It simmers over the trees, the horizon of the pines. It's in the air, warm and wet when I breathe.

If I imagine hard enough, I can see myself lifting into the air. I rise above the ground. Higher and higher until I can see the tops of the trees, and then the layout of the town, like a heart-shaped patch, a sea of green and gold cupped by a dark shadow of forest.

Acknowledgments

Thank you to my Vermont friends, Madison, Andrea, Stephanie, Liz, and Allison, for being the rocks I needed, for showing up during panic attacks, depressive lows, holding my hand, and encouraging me through the hard times.

Thank you to my friends who were there for me from afar that year in Vermont: Dan, Donna, Lisa, Susan, Vicki, Beth, and Mona. Thank you for your texts, calls, jokes, laughter, and love. I have never been more grateful to have such amazing people by my side rooting for me, near or far.

Thank you, my Bauer-Jones family. You guys are my WORLD. There was never a moment in Vermont where I felt alone, because I knew I had you. Thank you for being my family, my place to do laundry, my people to complain to, my spare bedroom, the parents of my god-doggies.

And to E., for giving me a reason to wake up in the morning when I needed it most.

BIOGRAPHICAL NOTE

CHELSEA CATHERINE is a PEN Short Story Prize Nominee, a winner of the Raymond Carver Fiction Contest in 2016, a Sterling Watson fellow, and an Ann McKee Grant recipient. Her novella *Blindsided* won the Clay Reynolds Novella Prize and was published in October of 2018. Her nonfiction recently won the Mary C. Mohr Award through the *Southern Indiana Review*. A native Vermonter, Catherine lived in Key West for two years where she was secretary of the Key West Writers Guild. She now lives in St. Petersburg, FL.